THE MALTA FRIGATE

By the same author

Seven Gun Broadside
The Quarterdeck Ladder
A Sword for Mr Fitton
Mr Fitton's Commission
The Baltic Convoy
A Kiss for Captain Hardy
Centurion Comes Home

and General Bonaparte had called on the Knights of Malta to surrender, which they had done after a most feeble resistance. The Frenchmen had raged through the *casals* gutting the great churches and smashing the holy images, stealing and destroying without restraint, for a fortnight; the Knights of St John – except some who were of the French Auberge and had welcomed the invaders – had all been shipped off to Italy when General Bonaparte and his fleet sailed away at the end of June.

As for the French soldiers, there was a garrison in the old fortified capital of Mdina and another on Gozo beyond the Komino strait, but all the rest were behind the walls of the Valletta forts with every sack of grain, every beast that would make meat, that the farmers and peasants had been unable to hide from them. Thieves, pagans, worse than the pirates of the Barbary coast –

Peard ceased to hear him. Two months ago the French fleet had sailed – had Nelson intercepted it? If there had been a battle that long ago the news would surely have spread by now. There was much else he wanted to know but his immediate needs were pressing.

'Water for the frigate,' he said sharply, interrupting a furious tirade against the heathen French. 'And new spars.'

Boney, having calmed himself with a visible effort, replied that his uncle had agreed to arrange the watering of the ship, though this would take several days. Additional casks would have to be found, with mule-carts and donkeys to transport them from the wells, but it would be done. The spars were more difficult. Only in Valletta dockyard, now in French possession, could such spars be found, and only one man – the Viconde, Boney called him – knew how to get them from under the noses of the French.

'We go now, sir, to see the Viconde,' Boney ended with satisfaction. 'My uncle take us in his *carrozza*.'

Peard frowned. 'Now? Where is this Viconde?'

'At Tal-Marfa, sir – two, three mile.' Outside in the square harness jingled and wheels ground to a halt. Boney tossed the contents of his glass down his throat and pointed to the captain's half-empty glass. 'Please finish, sir. We go.'

After a moment's hesitation Peard swallowed the rest of the fiery drink, making a mental note to see that none of his crew came within arm's-length of *mastica*, and went outside. The vehicle standing there looked in the dim light like a hearse. Kazan was on the box, and an undersized horse was between the shafts of what seemed to be an ancient four-wheeled carriage with a fringed canopy stretched above it like an awning. A strong smell of goat greeted him as he scrambled in. Boney, with a muttered apology, got in beside him, Kazan cracked his whip, and they trundled away.

Possibly the *mastica* had something to do with Peard's sudden access of confidence as the *carrozza* jolted its way out of the sleeping village of Bugibba. The situation on Malta was tricky but he looked like succeeding in his enterprise in spite of it. This promptness of action was a thing he had not before experienced in his dealings with the Mediterranean peoples and his heart warmed towards Boney and his uncle; if these were true samples of the Maltese folk he was sorry for their present plight – though indeed it was no worse than that of the other small countries under the French heel. The carriage was beginning to climb the long hill out of Bugibba, the way they had come.

'What manner of man is the Viconde you spoke of?' he demanded.

'A good man, very clever man,' said Boney out of the darkness; he paused, apparently to seek for words. 'A nobleman, of the blood of the Knights, but caring always for Malta and Maltese peoples, sir.'

'You said all the Knights were sent to Italy.'

Boney's explanation was hampered as much by the lurch and groan of the *carrozza* as by his limited vocabulary, but Peard gathered that the Viconde and his lady had been at their country house in the Gharghur hills when the French took Valletta; that they had hidden in a cave during the two weeks of French marauding, helped by Kazan and others; and

THE MALTA FRIGATE

SHOWELL STYLES

WILLIAM KIMBER · LONDON

First published in 1983 by
WILLIAM KIMBER & CO. LIMITED
100 Jermyn Street
London SW1Y 6EE

ISBN 0-7183-0439-X

M 63949

F

Photoset in North Wales by
Derek Doyle & Associates, Mold, Clwyd.
Printed in Great Britain by
Biddles Limited, Guildford.

Contents

Author's Note

Captain Shuldham Peard was a real person and the sea actions of the frigate *Success* are on record in James's *Naval History*.

CHAPTER ONE
Return to Malta

1

Captain Shuldham Peard, of His Majesty's 32-gun frigate *Success*, settled his rump on the vibrating wood of the crosstrees and hooked an arm round the topgallant mast. Close above his right shoulder the bellying canvas of the main royal rustled and tugged uneasily; there was barely enough wind to fill it. Down below his dangling white-stockinged legs the brown face of Rees, the lookout, peered up at him from the maintop, and down below Rees – another sixty feet down – was the frigate's deck with the foreshortened figures of seamen moving about their duties. He could see Wrench and Tildesley, second and third lieutenants, standing side by side staring up at him.

Peard's large brown face crinkled in a half-smile. He could sympathize with his lieutenants' anxiety. Their immediate future, perhaps their lives or deaths, depended upon what he saw from up here and what he decided to do about it. He clicked open his telescope with his left hand and steadied it on the horizon to westward.

A vast plain of dun-coloured sea under a low dun-coloured sky. The *khamsin* that had blown the frigate so far off course yesterday had robbed the blue Mediterranean of its rightful colour, and though its force had now dwindled to light southerly airs the sand it had lifted from the African deserts eighty leagues away still obscured the sun. The horizon was reasonably clear, though, and his glass showed him first the

three masts of a large vessel hull-down, with all sail set except
on the mainmast; that mainmast seemed to be no more than a
stump, with its rag of sail barely visible above the brown sea-
rim. He moved the glass a fraction to starboard, and gave an
involuntary grunt as the circle of the lens framed a second
vessel, a big frigate hull-up and almost dead ahead on his own
course. French, of course, with those triangular topsails. And
– Peard intensified his scrutiny for a long half-minute – he
knew her. Eighteen months ago he had chased that high stern
with its exaggerated tumblehome back into Toulon, and he'd
have known it anywhere.

He snapped the telescope shut, stuck it in his pocket, and
danced down the topgallant shrouds with a lightness
remarkable in so large a man. A nod to Rees sent the seaman
up to the crosstrees and Peard lowered himself through the
lubber's hole. A year or two ago he would have gone over the
edge of the top and down the futtock-shrouds like any young
topman. Now he would have considered such a thing an
unnecessary showing-off in a middle-aged post captain of four
years' seniority with an unblemished career in the Service and
a wife at home in Cornwall. And there was no point in
performing such feats for his own satisfaction, since he knew
his own capabilities and was perfectly contented with them.
Any spark of Celtic excitability inherited from his Cornish
father had long ago been quenched in the Saxon phlegm
bequeathed by his mother, a Gloucestershire lady, but there
was nevertheless a thrill of excitement in his breast as he
stepped down to the deck and turned an impassive
countenance on his waiting officers.

'Mr Wrench, I'll have the stuns'ls on her, if you please.'
Wrench, bullnecked and redfaced, touched his hat and ran
for'ard bellowing orders. 'Mr Tildesley,' added Peard, raising
his voice above the uproar, 'my compliments to Mr Fossett
and I'll be glad if he'll come on deck.'

'Aye aye, sir,' said Tildesley, blushing; he had been made
lieutenant only six weeks ago and still found it embarrassing
to be addressed politely.

Peard turned to go onto the quarterdeck. Behind him the surge of sound, fifty pairs of horny feet pounding across the deck, faded as the men raced up the shrouds to lay out on the yards. Just below him as he mounted the ladder the quartermaster beside the wheel released a different sequence of activity by turning the big watch-glass and nodding to the marine sentry on duty outside the door of the stern cabin. The marine tucked his musket against his side, took two clumping paces, and seized the clapper of the ship's bell to strike two double clangs. Instantly the quartermaster nodded to Quantrill, master's mate, who was ready with the reel of log-line at the break below the taffrail. Quantrill heaved the patent log overboard and the quartermaster squinted at the tiny sand-glass he had taken from his pocket.

'Turn! ... Stop!'

Quantrill nipped the line midway between two of its knots and chalked '3½ knots' on the logboard that hung below the rail. Peard gained his quarterdeck and began to walk up and down the weather side; Macaulay, the sailing-master, and West, the senior of his three midshipmen, were up there, but they had moved over to the lee rail, as naval usage required, as soon as he appeared. Four bells of the afternoon watch. Those studdingsails – they flapped and filled on the spars as he turned in his walk – might raise an extra knot for her, but they'd never catch *Diane* before nightfall unless she decided to stand and fight.

At the back of Peard's mind was the thought that it might be as well for *Success* if *Diane* did not so decide, but he could smother that thought without effort; since the age of twelve the Navy had taught him to think in terms of duty, not of opposing odds. He was perfectly sure that she was *Diane*, and almost as sure that she was engaged in escorting a damaged French ship-of-the-line to some safe haven – Toulon, most probably, now that De Brueys and his ships had got out of Toulon harbour and it was no longer blockaded. But if they were making for Toulon, what were the Frenchmen doing here, two hundred miles east-south-east of Malta, heading westward instead of nor'-nor' west for the Straits?

Fossett, first lieutenant, clattered up to the quarterdeck tugging the white lapels of his blue coat into place as he came. Peard returned his salute without pausing in his stride.

'We'll walk, Mr Fossett, if you please.'

They paced side by side, hands behind backs, turning inward like automatons at the end of each short march. Fossett was as tall as his senior but only half his breadth. His angular ascetic face gave him the look of a Methody parson, which belied his tyrannical nature. It had taken Peard a full year to teach Mr Fossett that discipline and efficiency did not depend on excessive flogging. Fossett heard his captain's brief account of his masthead observations without comment. He raised one bushy eyebrow at Peard's positive identification of *Diane* but knew better than to question it; for all his habitual amiability Peard was not the man to tolerate any demur from a subordinate.

'Ten miles ahead under plain sail,' Peard ended. 'If she doesn't run she'll be hull-up from the deck in half-an-hour.'

'And if she's in attendance on a dismasted seventy-four she won't run,' Fossett ruminated aloud. 'D'you reckon there's been a battle, sir?'

'Yesterday's gale could have brought down her mainmast.'

'Aye,' said Fossett. 'That – or Admiral Nelson, sir.'

They paced and turned in silence for a minute, the same thoughts in both their minds. A fortnight ago *Success* had returned to Gibraltar after an independent cruise only to be ordered to sea again immediately. Admiral de Brueys and his fifteen sail of the line, with 40,000 troops in transports, had sailed from Toulon for some unknown destination, and Rear-Admiral Sir Horatio Nelson's fleet of fourteen 74's was scouring the Mediterranean in search of them. Nelson was short of frigates and Peard's orders were to find and join him, no simple matter when Nelson might be anywhere on nearly a million square miles of sea.

The only two vessels he had spoken, a brig out of Ragusa and a Neapolitan snow, had seen nothing of either fleet, and this afternoon's sighting was the first indication of British or French presence in the eastern Mediterranean. The quick turn-round at Gibraltar had meant sailing with only half their water-casks filled and depriving the crew of their eagerly-anticipated shore leave; and it was this latter circumstance that prompted Fossett's next remark.

'An action just now, sir, would do us all the good in the world.'

Peard nodded agreement. 'Hands to witness punishment' had been piped three times in the past ten days. But at the back of his mind was the remembrance of *Diane*'s forty 18-pounders and his own 12-pounders, thirty-two of them, all as efficient as the maternal care of Mr Shorrocks the gunner could make them but none of them any younger than the very elderly *Success* herself.

'Deck! Frigate's hauled her wind, sir!'

Both officers halted as the lookout's hail came from the masthead. Peard stared ahead across the oily swell and then used his telescope. *Diane*'s upper sails were just in sight above the drab rim of the horizon, ranged now athwart his line of vision. She was going to fight. He looked round and his eye fell on Midshipman Hepplewhite, thirteen years old and small for his age – so small, indeed, that Peard hadn't seen him in the corner by the taffrail when he came on the quarterdeck.

'Signal midshipman! Make "enemy in sight".'

'Aye aye, sir,' squeaked Hepplewhite, and ran to the flag-locker.

No harm in suggesting for *Diane*'s benefit that he was signalling to a squadron below the horizon astern, though it was unlikely that Captain Gagneraud would believe it. He had heard of Jean Gagneraud as an excellent sea-officer and no fool.

'Now, Mr Fossett. Stuns'ls, royals and t'gallants off her. Then we'll beat to quarters.'

Fossett's tenor voice could carry like the squeal of a trumpet. Again the dark swarms of men surged up the shrouds; *Success*'s upper sails flapped, sagged, vanished; and before the last seaman had sprung down to the deck the startling *rat-a-tat-tat* of the drum rolled on upper and 'tween decks. To a pandemonium of thudding feet, shouted orders, and shrilling bosuns' pipes the frigate's deck filled with a seething mass of men weaving and jostling to get to their various stations. For a moment Peard had the quarterdeck to himself, and then with a multiple clatter and tramp the scarlet-and-white of the twenty marines filled the scanty space and the barked orders of Sergeant Ragg and Corporal Doherty added to the general uproar. Pressing himself against the taffrail out of their way, he watched critically while the last web of rope was stretched across between the shrouds to catch falling spars, the last hammock hurriedly shoved into the netting under the rail, and the last section of cabin-partition taken below to be stowed in the hold.

With dramatic suddenness the clamour was stilled, leaving in the silence a solitary voice that said, 'Shut your bloody – ' and stopped. Fossett came to the foot of the ladder and saluted. 'Cleared for action, sir.' Lieutenant Jacques of the marines, point-device even unto white gloves, clicked his heels. 'Marine detachment present and correct, sir.'

'Thank you,' Peard said. 'At ease, Mr Jacques. Mr Fossett, all guns load with ball.'

A new noise now, a stirring thunder as thirty-two gun-trucks rumbled inboard for the 12-pounders to be loaded and run out. Here was Fossett, reporting that last order executed. Then silence again except for the rustle and creak of the frigate's slow progress and a hushed buzz of voices – an occasional chuckle, too – from the waiting gun-crews. *Diane* was hull-up now, her foretopsail backed, presenting her larboard side towards him. With the telescope he could see the twenty open gunports of her broadside; those 18-pounders could rake him minutes before his own guns were within long range. He scanned the hundred yards of deck below him: Macauley beside the helmsman, carpenter's and bosun's parties in position, the gun-crews a perspective of brown-skinned groups with the junior officers in charge of their divisions –

Peard's ranging glance halted at number four division, the after guns starboard side. Midshipman Hepplewhite was nominally in charge of that division, and Midshipman Hepplewhite was plainly in a sorry state. His small face was greenish-white and his teeth were clenched on his lower lip, which even so was wobbling piteously. Peard could remember the dreadful minutes before his own first action at sea; he had been twelve years old.

'Mr Hepplewhite!' The boy jumped and turned a terrified face. 'Pray join me on the quarterdeck.' Hepplewhite scrambled up the ladder. 'We'll walk, if you please.'

They began to pace up and down, the midshipman's cocked hat on a level with his captain's epaulette and his short legs scuttling to keep up. The grins of the marines ranged along the quarterdeck rail vanished instantly as Peard glanced at them.

'You joined us at Gibraltar, Mr Hepplewhite, so you're not familiar with yonder Frenchman as the rest of us are.' Peard's tone was brisk and genial. 'On blockade duty we came to know the enemy's vessels pretty well. *Success* was with Sir James Saumarez' squadron off Toulon, you understand. Well, *Diane*, captain Jean Gagneraud – that's the fellow ahead of us – put her nose out of Toulon one day and got as far as the Porquerolles before we cut her off. She wouldn't stand and fight then, Mr Hepplewhite, so we chased her back into Toulon harbour.'

He forebore to mention that as Saumarez' 74's were in full view five miles to windward *Diane* had no option but to run for it. Colour was returning patchily to Mr Hepplewhite's cheeks. A glance ahead as they turned showed the French frigate nearer, waiting, almost motionless on the dun-coloured sea. Ten minutes more, or thereabouts.

'I fancy she'll fight now, however,' he went on cheerfully. 'You've been told her force, no doubt?'

'F-forty eighteen-pounders, sir.' Hepplewhite, forced to reply, gained confidence thereby. 'West said she'd b-blow us out of the water before we could come near her, sir.'

'Mr West is what Mr Coleridge the poet would call a

pessimist, Mr Hepplewhite. We shall probably have to stand
fire until our guns are in range, but Captain Gagneraud will
certainly aim high to try and disable our rigging.' *Diane* was
less than two miles away now. 'You had better go to your
station,' Peard said. 'And Mr Hepplewhite – I rely upon you
to see that the powder-boys don't lag, bringing up the
cartridges.'

'Aye aye, sir,' squeaked Hepplewhite, much encouraged,
and ran down the ladder to his place.

Success moved steadily on across the narrowing space of
water towards the long brown hull with its black row of
gunports. There was no talking at the guns now.

'Mr Fossett,' said Peard, 'we shall fire the starboard
broadside first. Full elevation.'

The words were hardly out of his mouth when *Diane*'s side
vanished in rolling clouds of smoke pierced by tongues of
yellow flame. Overhead the air shook with the shrill passage of
shot and the irregular thunder of the discharge followed on the
instant. No hit on the hull – his prediction had been correct –
but main and topsails on all three masts showed rents and he
could see a lot of severed cordage dangling on the foremast.
No spars gone, no one hurt. *Success* held on her uninterrupted
course, closing the distance – hardly extreme 12-pounder
range yet but it would steady his men to let them reply.

'Larboard, hard over,' he called down to the helmsman.
'Guns to fire as they bear, Mr Fossett.'

The frigate swung slowly towards the wind. The ear-
splitting bang of the for'ard 12-pounder was followed by the
successive explosions of the rest of the starboard broadside,
the acrid smoke drifting aft past Peard as he watched with his
telescope for the fall of shot. He saw a white splash or two, all
short, before the smoke and flame of *Diane*'s second broadside
spouted. Again she had fired high, and this time to more
effect. Amid the snap and twang of parted rigging there was a
splintering crash and above him the mizen topsail yard bent
like a wishbone and hung with its canvas flapping. A chorus of
yells sent his glance for'ard and he was just in time to see a

curious thing. A ball had struck the crosstrees at the base of the fore topgallant mast and completely severed it; every strand of its supporting rigging must have been cut, for the heavy spar leapt clear in mid-air and – still upright – plunged like a spear straight down on the foredeck with an impact that shook the frigate's hull. Her sail-trim disorganised, *Success* had turned right into the wind and was in stays, with Fossett yelling for hands to man the braces and get her back on course. Peard spun round to look at *Diane*; and his big hands tightened on the rails as he looked.

The French frigate was making sail. As the topgallants and royals drooped and filled on the yards she turned away from her antagonist and began to diminish westward towards the ship she was escorting. Down on deck the men were cheering and he could hear Hepplewhite's shrill treble huzza-ing with the rest, but Peard was smouldering with anger though his impassive face showed nothing of it. This was no triumph. Doubtless the damaged 74 had signalled for her protector to break off the action and rejoin her; doubtless that had saved his outgunned vessel from a desperate battle. But there was a sort of contempt here – two well-aimed broadsides and no need for more – that he found galling. He would have liked to kick Captain Gagneraud's backside. Then he chuckled inwardly at his own unreasonableness and turned his usual goodhumoured countenance to the lieutenant of marines.

'I believe you may dismiss your men, Mr Jacques,' he said, and went for'ard to assess the damage.

2

'Broster reckons he can fish the yard, sir,' said Fossett, 'but the fallen t'garn mast's sprung and we've no replacement.'

'We ought to be able to get a thirty-foot spar when we reach Alexandria,' Peard said reflectively.

'Three hundred leagues,' growled the sailing master, rolling the r's. 'That's a fair wee distance, sir. It's but sixty leagues to

Malta, and mayhap the Knights would find one for us.'

They were conferring in the captain's day-cabin. Their late antagonist and her charge had vanished over the western horizon an hour ago and *Success*, hove-to on an empty sea, had nearly finished repairing her damage. A brisk hammering sounded for'ard where Mr Neal and his party were completing a temporary repair to the splintered gash in the foredeck made by the plunging topgallant mast. Here was the weakest part of the old frigate's ageing timbers, and the planking was to have been renewed at Gibraltar had there been time; the butt of the mast had smashed clean through into the upper forehold, where the water-casks had been stowed by the captain's order to bring her a little more by the head, and shattered one of the three casks. The falling mast had also broken a man's arm – the only casualty of the abortive engagement. The loss of the water-cask meant half-rations or less until they watered at Alexandria.

'If Nelson's anywhere he must be east'rd of us, sir,' Fossett said. 'In putting back for Malta we'll lose a deal of distance.'

Peard nodded. 'That's true. On the other hand – pray come in, Mr Gubbins. You've something to report?'

The purser, a little ferret-faced man, entered hesitantly and gulped before he spoke. 'Sir, Mr Wrench's respects and we can make sail when you wish.'

'Very good, Mr Gubbins. Thank you.'

Gubbins shifted his feet and swallowed twice. 'There's something else, sir. The water. I tapped the remaining two casks and they're foul, sir. Not just green – thick foul. A pig couldn't drink it, sir.'

'Are you telling us you didn't sample it at Gibraltar?' snarled the first lieutenant, his thin face reddening.

'There wasn't time,' Gubbins muttered.

'By God, Mr Purser, it's your duty to make time! Damned slackness is what I'd call it, and if you've no better idea of your duty than – '

He checked himself as Peard held up a hand.

'We've a barrel or two of small beer left, I believe,' Peard said. 'Bring me an account of them, Mr Gubbins, if you please. – Well, gentlemen,' he continued as the purser hurried out, 'that solves our problem for us. Mr Macaulay, I'll thank you to lay me a course for Malta.'

Half-an-hour later, with *Success* heading westward under her reduced sail, he could hand over to Fossett and pass the word for his steward.

'A glass of wine and a biscuit in my cabin, Boney,' he said when the little man came running aft.

'Yassir,' said Boney with a flash of white teeth, and rolled away with the speed and smoothness of a ball.

There were many Maltese among the dozen or so different nationalities serving in the Mediterranean Fleet and Boney was one of them. His proper name was Bonici and the nickname was inevitable, but it was singularly unsuited to his plump rotundity or to his violent hatred of the French.

Peard sat at the table in his day-cabin to write the Log entry. It was already headed *Thursday August 30 1798* and was inscribed with details of winds, latitude and longitude, and distance run in the forenoon. He wrote: *At 2 sighted two sail 11 miles, W, and gave chase*, and paused, frowning. It wasn't going to be a very creditable entry and had better be made as brief as possible. He laid down his pen again as Boney came in with wine and ship's biscuit on a tray.

'Tell me, Boney,' he said, tapping the hard-tack on the table out of habit, 'where do you get your water on Malta?'

The island was a mere lump of limestone, he remembered, with not a river anywhere.

'Wells, sir,' grinned Boney. '*Molinos* – windmills.'

Of course. Artesian wells as he might have known. He dismissed the steward, finished the Log entry with help from the wine, and went into his sleeping-cabin. The wind had freshened slightly, tempering the heat of an August afternoon in *khamsin* weather, but it was hot in the little cabin. Peard threw off his blue coat and loosened his stock before lying down on the palliasse of his folding cot. For once there was no immediate problem of ship management to occupy his mind and he could let his thoughts go free. They flew at once to Malta.

Nineteen years ago, 1779, and he had never been there since. Valletta was not a port used by the Navy, whose main base east of the Rock was Port Mahon in Minorca. Why *Zealous* had called there he had never discovered; some political matter, or just to show the Flag – a gawky midshipman of nineteen wouldn't know or care. But the Grand Master of the Knights had ordained a banquet for the officers of *Zealous*, and Captain Rowe had included his senior midshipman in the party. Peard could picture the glittering scene now: the great hall hung with tapestries and trophies, the black-and-silver robes of the Knights of St John, the gold plates piled with exotic dishes, the bejewelled women with powdered hair. And Julia.

Maybe some major domo had arranged that they should be seated together because Julia spoke English; an odd sort of English in a voice surprisingly deep and sweet for a girl of fifteen. French was her normal speech, however, and since young Peard was fluent in it they had talked English and French as they felt inclined. She was a Boisredin, she told him proudly, her father a Knight of the Auberge de Provence, and her mother – dead these many years – had been a Scottish lady of title, very beautiful and with many lovers. That, and some of Julia's eager questions, had somewhat shocked young Peard. Did he keep a mistress on board that big ship? How many women did the captain have? Was it true that sailors were the most exciting *amorosos*? But successive glasses of excellent wine had made this lickerish preoccupation increasingly attractive, and they had chattered and laughed together in a quite disgraceful manner until the lordly meal had ended and their seniors were moving towards a vast withdrawing room. Then (his recollection of how it came about was misty) there was the darkened room and the couch, the warm and scented air full of hair-powder and garments madly flung aside, the panting encounter, the stinging ecstasy ...

Nineteen years ago. He had seen her only once more after she had left him; a demure maiden curtseying composedly with the other ladies as the British officers took their leave. And for a full month after *Zealous*'s sailing he had suffered the most terrible pangs of frustrated love; had planned to desert at Mahon, to steal a cutter and sail back to Valletta. Young fool! Well, it had passed and there had been other girls, though none so vividly remembered. Other loves too – ships and the sea, books, music, the Service. And Lucy, in a special way. They had married as soon as he had been made post and could afford the small manor-house on the hill above Penryn. The last time he had seen Lucy little Tom had been eight months old; he'd be two years and a month now, trotting and tumbling on the green slopes below the house. The green slopes and the grey house with the latticed windows were in Peard's mind as he drifted into sleep.

Before nightfall the wind backed easterly, a fresh breeze banishing the last of the *khamsin* haze. Peard, on deck for the four hours of the middle watch, walked his quarterdeck beneath a clear sky ablaze with stars and kept a quick ear and a lifting eye for the straining canvas overhead; he had risked topgallants and royals on main and mizen, and so far Mr Broster's splicing of the damaged stays and shrouds had held. By morning a strong north-easter was raising whitecaps on a dark-blue sea – a 'grigal', Boney declared when he brought the captain his breakfast – and *Success* had to take in sail. Even so she was making 8½ knots with that quartering wind and should raise the Malta coast before dusk if it held. Hold it did, and a little after two bells on the second dog-watch the lookout hailed the deck with 'Land right ahead!' Half-an-hour later a rind of palest gold could be seen from the quarterdeck, seeming to rest on the hard blue bar of the horizon.

'A good landfall, Mr Macaulay,' said Peard.

The sailing-master grunted. 'Yon's Delimara Point. Ye'll need to bear up half-a-point to clear Il Gzira, sir.'

Peard called his orders to Wrench, who had the deck, and with much cheerful yo-ho-ing from the watch-on-deck (a run

ashore in prospect after all) the yards were braced round a
trifle and *Success*'s long bowsprit swung until it was pointing
well to the right of the distant segment of coast.

There was a stir of excitement in Peard's breast as he stood
at the quarterdeck rail and watched the island's south-east
coast grow out of the sea; a feeling more apt to a romantic
midshipman than to a middle-aged post captain. He felt, as he
had felt all those years ago, that he was approaching a place
magical and apart, remote from the modern world. Here was
an island no bigger than the Isle of Wight that was yet a
nation with its own language, older than Rome; a nation
despotically ruled by a mediaeval nobility who claimed
descent from the Crusader Knights of St John and whose feats
of arms against the Barbary pirates were legendary. It was as
if a living portion of history had been preserved and isolated in
the great Sea between Europe and Africa, away from the
eighty-year-old conflict in which all the northern nations were
engaged and clear of the sea-routes used by their warships.
Doubtless the régime of the present Knights Hospitallers was
tyrannical; doubtless they were (as he had heard) decadent
and immoral. Yet the glamour remained of a place unique, a
sea-girt fortress for centuries unchanged.

Two miles away on the larboard beam the low rocky coast
glowed red-gold as the frigate trimmed her sails to a soldier's
wind and flew north-westward. A village on a hilltop inland –
a cluster of stone houses and a huge church dome – shone like
an outpost of Eldorado. Dropping his gaze, Peard saw that his
steward was standing at the larboard rail, motionless, staring
avidly at the coast, and reflected that it must be some years
since Boney had seen his native land. But now the coast was
opening in the twin gaps of the Valletta harbours; Grand
Harbour, he remembered, was the English version of the
name of the deeply-cut southern inlet.

'Hands to sheets and braces! Helm a-larboard – steady as
she goes. Signal midshipman, hoist the colours, all of them.'

The British flag was flying at yardarm, main, and the
stump of the foremast as *Success* made in towards the land. The

first lieutenant had come up and most of the watch-below were crowded on the foredeck, gazing at the mighty defences built two centuries ago by Grand Master La Vallette to make his harbour of Valletta impregnable to assault. The huge limestone walls, washed a deep pink by the last light of the sinking sun, rose on either side of the harbour entrance as imposingly as the cliffs of Dover, Fort Ricasoli to larboard and Fort St Elmo to starboard. With his telescope Peard could discern the intricacies of bastion and demi-bastion, curtain and ravelin and lunette. His eye was on the crenellations on the battlements of St Elmo when they were hidden by a puff of white smoke.

'These Knights have pretty manners,' Fossett observed. 'A salute while we're still – '

'See there,' Peard cut him short, pointing.

A musket-shot away on the beam a tall column of white rose from the waves and subsided.

'Sixty-four pounder, or I'm a Dutchman!' shouted Fossett angrily. 'What in hell do they think we are?'

Peard's telescope was at his eye again. He focussed it carefully on the flag that streamed from its staff above Fort St Elmo. Two more white puffs broke from the battlements as he looked.

'That's the Tricouleur up there, Mr Fossett,' he said evenly.

The crescendo whir-r-r of a heavy shot passing overhead came on the heels of his words, the ball dropping well astern, and another white fountain spurted close on the frigate's starboard quarter. Peard was at the taffrail, his deep voice ringing urgently.

'All hands! 'Bout ship, and lively!'

Fossett, trumpeting shrilly, bolted down to the deck where Wrench and Tildesley and the petty officers were hounding the men to sheets and braces. Round spun *Success*, turning on her heel with leaning masts, to beat away close-hauled on the starboard tack, while two more shots from the fort's guns plunged almost together into the creaming swirl of her wake. A sixth shot, which proved to be the last, fell much farther astern though still in line. As the frigate steadied on her course nor'-west and the deck watch settled into their usual places below the rail the forts of Valletta were like two glowing rubies in the sunset light, dwindling astern beyond the darkening sea. With the coming of night the wind fell away to a light breeze, and by then the island of Malta was invisible under the immense dome of stars.

Peard ordered the frigate hove-to under main and topsails, spread the chart (Condry's of 1792) on the table below the hanging lantern, and shouted for his steward to bring him coffee. He stared unseeing at the chart for a moment. He might contrive to continue the voyage to Alexandria with his damaged spars, but water they must have, and quickly. Through the Messina strait to Palermo was a four-day voyage, more if this north-easter continued to blow; Cape Passero was only a hundred miles north, but if he was lucky enough to find a stream on the Sicilian coast where he could fill his casks he had only two sound casks to fill. And Malta was at hand, close under his lee. Why the island should have declared for France he couldn't imagine – though indeed some few of the Knights were of French descent – but at least he knew now where *Diane* and the French 74 had been making for. They were safely in Grand Harbour. They must have known weeks ago, then, that Malta had taken sides against the British. And that meant –

'Coffee, sir,' said his steward.

'Thank you,' Peard said absently, taking the steaming mug; but Boney made no move to go. 'Well, what is it?'

'Sir, Melita not French!' Boney got out, like an explosion. 'Maltese never go along with bloody Frogs, sir – never, never!'

Peard checked the reprimand he was about to utter. The little man's words chimed with an underthought of his own.

'Valletta fired on us, Boney,' he said quietly, 'and the French flag was flying on St Elmo.'

Boney's round dark face was deadly serious and his black eyes flashed. 'Why, I not know. I telling you, sir – all the true Maltese hate the French same's me.' He leaned forward. 'Sir, I pray you to listen me. You wish water, you wish spars. On

Malta you get water and spars – I know to get them.'

'How?' demanded Peard sharply.

'Sir, I am man of Bugibba and all know me. By Bugibba is Salina Bay seven mile to north of Valletta, where I was fisherman. Ten fathom, sir, half-mile out – '

'Show me,' said Peard.

They bent over the chart together.

3

Seated in the sternsheets of the cutter with a hand on the tiller, Peard watched the black outline of the cliffs on either hand rising against the stars as the inlet narrowed ahead. Across the inky surface the shore-scent drifted to his nostrils, a mingling of rotting fish and wild thyme. The dip and plash of the eight oars working in muffled rowlocks was the only sound except for the faint wash of small waves on the rocks at the feet of the cliffs.

'More starboard, sir,' said Boney's low voice close to his left knee. 'Salt-pans larboard, sir.'

Tildesley's sword-hilt nudged Peard's side as the third lieutenant shifted on the stern-thwart to look leftward. Just visible in the starshine, a long flat shelf of rock, almost awash, slid past a biscuit-toss from the boat, its surface showing a regular pattern of white patches – the salt-pans that gave Salina Bay its name, Peard assumed. He glanced astern. *Success* was still clearly visible in black outline, lying at anchor in ten fathoms between the two headlands; much too visible. But there had been no alarm, not a single light on shore as she crept in from northward and rounded-to under Boney's direction, no challenge from the squat towers that topped the cliffs on either side of the bay's narrow entrance. The towers, Boney had told him, were little more than ruins, built two centuries ago to watch for the galleys of the Algerine corsairs. He smiled wryly in the darkness, reflecting how completely this expedition was in the hands of a captain's steward. Boney had been valued because he was an excellent servant and always cheerful; now he was in effect pilot and chief adviser, with the safety of *Success* and her people in his hands. The little man had taken on a new stature.

Ahead the rock walls of the inlet were fast narrowing. The Maltese rose from his crouching position against the gunwale to peer across the bows. Peard tapped his arm and told him to take the tiller.

It had not been easy to decide what form this landing should take, for there was no certainty that the steward's assertions were correct; the events at Valletta more than hinted that this was an enemy coast, where a landing would be opposed and he and his men captured. In the end he had resolved to risk as little as possible: four seamen, third lieutenant in charge of the cutter, Boney and himself, cutlasses and pistols as a mere precaution. Boney had warned that they might have to spend some hours ashore so he had ordered Fossett to stand by with the frigate in a state of full preparedness and arranged a signal code with blue-lights. If he had not returned by sunrise *Success* was to up-anchor and make for the coast of Sicily.

'No oars, sir, please,' said Boney.

' 'Vast pulling,' growled Peard. 'Bows.'

The cutter glided in between low cliffs, the channel here no more than a dozen fathoms wide, until her forefoot ground gently into a shingle slope where the dim shapes of small boats lay pulled up. The seaman in the bows jumped over into the shallows to hold her while Peard stepped ashore.

'Very well, Mr Tildesley. Back you go.'

'Aye aye, sir. And – good luck, sir.'

'Bugibba twenty minutes, sir,' muttered Boney at his side, slinging the satchel of blue-lights on his shoulder.

'Lead on,' said Peard.

They toiled upward between the black shapes of boulders still warm from yesterday's sun to a little path that mounted through thickets of bamboo-grass to the cliff-top. Peard had sweated on the rough ascent and the faint northerly breeze was welcome. Behind and below him on the dark glimmer of Salina Bay he could see the frigate quite plainly, with the black dot of the cutter moving towards her, and for a moment he felt cut-off and oddly awkward; a sea officer detached from his ship was like a cavalryman deprived of his horse. But Boney was leading the way across a ridge of arid rock and the prospect on its farther side was opening below – the much wider bay to the west of the Salina. From his study of the chart he knew it had a shoal at its entrance and an island where (it was said) the Apostle Paul had been shipwrecked in Anno Domini 58. A wider and very dusty track underfoot now, winding downhill.

'That way Valletta,' said Boney, jerking his thumb leftward. 'Very near Bugibba now, sir.'

The track slanted down rocky hillside where the fragrance of thyme drifted in the warm air. The white radiance of starlight revealed terraced fields on either hand, a cluster of square stone houses close above the shore of the bay. The smell of excrement, human and animal, took the place of the thyme-scent as they passed between the first silent and lightless dwellings of the village and somewhere a horse whinnied and snorted. The squat figure of the Maltese trotted confidently ahead, through a dark and twisting alley to a small unpaved square surrounded by somewhat bigger houses on three sides, the fourth side being occupied by the porch and tower of a large church.

Boney crossed the empty square with Peard at his heels and stopped before the door of the house opposite the church porch. His knock on the door echoed loudly in the silence and involuntarily the Englishman laid a hand on his sword-hilt and glanced quickly round him. It took two more knockings to produce any response. A glimmer of light showed in the door-jamb, a man's voice made gruff demand which Boney answered with an unintelligible flood of words.

There was a loud ejaculation, the rasp of bolts as the door was flung open, and they were drawn into a low, whitewashed room with a flagged floor, where the man who had admitted them set his lantern on the table and clasped the little steward to his bosom. He was bearded and broad-shouldered, and the blue shirt he had hastily flung across his shoulders revealed a chest covered with hair as black and thickly-curled as the thatch on Boney's head. Boney extricated himself and waved a hand.

'Hannibal Kazan, my uncle – chief man of Bugibba,' he said with some pride. 'Captain Peard of His Britannic Majesty's frigate *Success*.'

Kazan stuck out a horny fist. '*Sahha*,' he said heartily. 'English. *Sahha*.'

From a wall cupboard he took a bottle and glasses and deftly poured a drink for each of them. He gestured to Peard to sit in the only chair at the table, raised his glass in salute, and turned to his nephew.

'Ask him,' began Peard; but they were already at it hammer-and-tongs, a dual torrent of words rising in a spate of excitement.

He could only sit back and sip his drink, a colourless liquid that tasted like raw alcohol flavoured with aniseed, watching the interplay of flailing gesture and head-shaking, unable even to guess the meaning of words that had no roots in common with any European language. Again he realised how totally dependent he was upon Boney, but he was less worried than he might have been; the past few hours had discovered capabilities in Taddeo Bonici that hadn't been suspected by his captain. At the speed these two were talking, he told himself, the colloquy shouldn't take long. It ended abruptly with Kazan, pausing only to throw a grin and a rapid gesture at the captain, dashing out through an inner door.

'Now then,' said Peard as Boney turned to face him.

Excitement and the desire for rapid utterance made the steward's English hard to understand and he had to be halted more than once, but the story that emerged was an arresting one. There was a French army in Valletta – an army of 4,000 soldiers with a general named Vaubois. Ten weeks ago a great fleet of warships and transports had appeared off the island

that they were now back at Tal-Marfa, where – if Peard understood him correctly – the Viconde was planning some sort of action against the invaders.

'Very clever man,' Boney said again. 'He speak Italian, English, French – '

'He speaks English?' Another burden lifted from Peard's mind. 'In that case – '

He stopped in order to extricate himself from Boney, who had been flung on top of him by the violent swaying of the carriage. They had reached the top of the hill and Kazan had whipped his horse into a shambling gallop that seemed likely to disintegrate the ancient vehicle if it didn't overturn it first. Peard would have been happier in a cockboat among Atlantic rollers. Clinging grimly to the side of the *carrozza* he stared out at a starlit landscape dimly and intermittently visible beyond clouds of white dust. They were bucketing across an uneven plateau where dark rock-outcrops reared between little stone-walled fields, on a road (if it could be called that) no more than a stony track winding between piles of boulders.

They rattled down into what seemed to be a dry watercourse, toiled out on the other side, and came to more level ground with a wall of black crags above it on their left. The faint scent of trees and plants came to Peard's nostrils as the carriage passed between the pillars of a gateless entrance beyond which a row of outhouses or stables stood at the base of the crags. He had time to reflect that the Viconde was less likely than Boney's uncle to relish being knocked-up at something after one o'clock in the morning, and then the carriage stopped before the stone porch of a considerable two-storey mansion.

Someone was up and about in the house, for a yellow radiance shone from a downstairs window. Its light glinted on the musket and bandolier of the man who stepped forward as Peard and the steward got out. After a brief exchange of question and answer with Boney this sentry led them into a stone-flagged hall, knocked respectfully on a door at the side, and in response to a sharp order from the man within threw it open to admit them.

The room was small, lit by a branch of four candles above the paper-littered table where a man was sitting. He was in shirt and breeches, for the room was hot, but the shirt was of fine linen with a frilled bosom. A grey scratch-wig was perched askew on top of a bald dome of head, and a nose like an eagle's beak enhanced the bird-of-prey impression produced by a darting turn of the head as the visitors entered. While Boney poured out a flood of explanation in Maltese, two penetrating grey eyes under fiercely-sprouting brows surveyed the frigate captain's big figure from ruffled black hair to dusty buckled shoes. He rose to his feet, cut short the steward's volubility and dismissed him from the room in one expressive gesture, and held out a long thin hand.

'You are most welcome on this island, Captain Peard. There is a chair beside you – pray be seated.'

Except for a very precise pronunciation his English was excellent. Much relieved, Peard sat down.

'Thank you – er – Viconde. You must forgive me,' he added with a smile, 'if I don't address you correctly. Bonici, my steward, is my only guide in the matter.'

'Let us dispense with ceremony, captain.' There was no answering smile in the austere, deeply-lined face. 'I am busy, as you see. Two points. Firstly, I have abjured the title. I am Emmanuele Vitale, lately notary-justiciar in Valletta. Secondly, Bonici has apprised me of your situation but I wish an account of it in your own language.'

'It'll be a pleasure to use it again, believe me, sir,' Peard said, 'especially to one who speaks it as well as you do.'

Vitale flicked a finger impatiently. 'I hold my law degree from the University of Cambridge. Before my marriage I was three years in England and am fortunate in that my wife also speaks your tongue. Now, captain, speak – and please to be concise.'

'I'll do my best,' said Peard, a trifle nettled. 'My frigate is the *Success* of thirty-two guns. She's at anchor in the mouth of Salina Bay – ' He checked himself and turned in his chair as the door behind him opened.

A woman stood in the doorway, a candlestick with lighted candle in one hand and the other holding the folds of the silken embroidered shawl draped round her shoulders. Long dark hair hanging in disarray framed a lovely face, heart-shaped, flushed with sleep. Like a sudden chord of music heard from far away, remembrance stirred in the depths of Peard's mind. Of course it couldn't be. This wasn't the slim girl of the banquet in Valletta, who had – Impossible. And yet –

Vitale, who had begun to speak angrily in Maltese, stopped and spoke in English.

'You should not be here,' he said sternly. 'I wish to be private, Julia.'

CHAPTER TWO
Dangerous Anchorage

1

'I heard a carriage,' said Julia Vitale in hesitant English, looking at Peard. 'Your visitor, Emmanuele, is an English – ' she paused, seeking a word – *'capitaine de vaisseau*, I think?'

Beneath the embroidered shawl she wore a nightrail of white silk and her feet in scarlet mules peeped from under its hem. If the Julia of long ago had been Diana, Peard was thinking, this was Juno, full-bosomed and lovely. He rose to his feet.

'Captain Peard of the frigate *Success*,' Vitale growled reluctantly. 'My wife, the Lady Julia.'

Peard bowed. Julia sketched a curtsey. Then she looked up at him, her brown eyes wide.

'Peard? Was there not a – a midshipman, of a ship called *Zealous* – '

'The same, ma'am,' said Peard, smiling. 'I'm honoured by your remembrance of him.'

Vitale, frowning, glanced quickly from one to the other. 'You have met before?'

'A score of years ago, sir,' Peard said. 'As children, you might say.'

His eyes were on Julia as he spoke and he saw the small mischievous smile at one corner of her red mouth where a dimple lurked. He remembered both smile and dimple from that earlier encounter; she wasn't greatly changed, it appeared.

'Captain Peard has urgent business to transact,' her husband said curtly. 'You will please to leave us.'

She threw a disdainful glance at him and a smile at the captain. 'We shall meet again, Captain Peard. *A bientôt.*'

'I have to apologise for this interruption,' Vitale said irritably as the door closed behind her. 'My household is disarranged lately. My wife, also, is not herself. Her father, Boisredin, was among the renegade Knights who welcomed the French when Valletta was surrendered.'

'And you alone of the – um – loyal Knights escaped capture?' Peard said, reseating himself. 'I'm told you hid in a cave – '

'I am not of the Knights of Malta, Captain Peard!' Vitale snapped angrily. 'Nor am I for them. These French dogs have benefited us Maltese by ridding us of their antiquated tyranny. We shall never permit a return to it. Here – ' he waved a hand at the paper-strewn table – 'I begin the work of making the Maltese a nation. The future – but this is not to the point.' He passed a hand across his forehead. 'Your frigate is anchored in Salina Bay. Pray continue.'

He listened attentively and without comment while Peard, remembering the adjuration to conciseness, explained his situation. Then he pushed paper, quill, and inkwell towards him.

'Dimensions of the spars required.' His tone had regained its original cold precision. 'We shall try to get them for you. It may take time.'

'How long, sir?'

'That is impossible to say. You are aware of our position – our only port and dockyard in enemy hands. A raid will have to be planned, men who know the dockyard selected, a reconnaissance made. This cannot be done in a day, or two days.'

'I understand,' said Peard, handing over his note of dimensions. 'And as to payment – '

'No payment, Captain Peard, but a *quid pro quo*. I ask you in return to aid us with your frigate in our struggle against the

French.' Vitale raised a hand as the captain started to speak. 'Attend, please. In Valletta is this General Vaubois with four thousand soldiers, in Mdina a garrison of five hundred, in Mgiarr fortress on Gozo Island two hundred more. My information, which is sure, is that they have thirty thousand muskets and twelve thousand barrels of powder. The great guns of the fortresses are under their hand. When I have completed these lists – ' he tapped a sheaf of papers in front of him – 'they will record the names of fifteen hundred Maltese fighters. We have thirty-four muskets and shotguns and no artillery. But we shall fight, captain, and with you to help us – '

'That's impossible,' Peard interrupted firmly. 'I'm under orders, sir. I've a duty to perform.'

The Viconde's dark eyes flashed. 'Is it not your duty to attack the French wherever you find them?'

'Yes – but under the authority of my senior officers. I'm ordered by them to seek out Admiral Nelson and attach my ship to his fleet. If I don't obey to the best of my ability I'm subject to the death penalty – by the law of my Service. But this I can promise,' Peard went on quickly, forestalling a reply. 'When I take *Success* away from here I'll use every endeavour to get help sent to Malta as soon as possible. Admiral Nelson will act, depend upon it, as soon as he knows what's afoot.'

Vitale stared at him for a moment under lowered brows. In the brief silence the buzzing of the flies that occupied every corner of the room sounded unnaturally loud.

'I must agree,' he said abruptly. 'You shall have your spars, captain. I know where your ship is lying and will inform you by messenger when I have them.'

'You know where my ship is lying,' Peard echoed with a sudden frown. 'So will a good many of your people. If one of them were to inform the French – '

'There are no informers among us, Captain Peard!' the Viconde broke in with another flash of anger. 'Clearly you have no conception of Malta. For every man, woman and child here the Church is synonymous with God. The French have desecrated our churches, their nation has renounced God, and every Frenchman is Anti-Christ with hell-fire a certainty for any man who aids him. A deed shall be done in two days' time that will show — ' He stopped himself, frowning, and went on more quietly. 'As to informers, however, I have my own within the walls of Valletta. The news they send is reliable. I can tell you, for example, that the frigate *Justice* in Valletta harbour was joined yesterday by another frigate, the *Diane*, and a line-of-battle ship lacking mast, the *Guillaume Tell*.'

So the 'damaged 74' sighted by *Success* was an 80-gun ship from De Brueys's Toulon fleet. Where was the rest of it? Had Nelson met them? Peard thought of the two frigates, one of them at least fit for sea, and frowned.

'Don't the French send out patrols?' he asked.

Vitale shook his head. 'Not since those first two weeks of rapine. Why should they? They have pillaged every church, taken every weapon and every *cantar* of grain they could find. And there are women enough for them in Valletta and the Three Cities,' he added bitterly.

Peard was not content. If the French took it into their heads to send *Diane* on an inshore patrol of the coast she could hardly miss *Success*, anchored out there between the headlands. A lee shore, too, with this northerly breeze –

He got to his feet. 'Thank you, sir, for your promised help. There'll be a *quid pro quo* in due course, I assure you.'

Vitale had not smiled once during their interview nor did he smile as he briefly grasped the captain's outstretched hand. Though the room was stifling hot his thin fingers were fish-cold.

'You will do what you can,' he said absently; already, it was plain, his thoughts were back among the sea of papers on the table. 'God go with you, captain.'

In the dark hallway the sentry was waiting to conduct Peard outside to where Boney and his uncle stood talking in low voices beside the *carrozza*. He sniffed the air and cast a glance at the starry sky before getting in, sensing an imminent change of wind, and the glance showed him a lit upper window and a black silhouette – the Lady Julia, doubtless. She had stirred his senses, he admitted to himself with a frown as the carriage rattled out through the gateway; it was a trifle disturbing to find that there was some of the riggish young midshipman in the middle-aged post captain yet. As for her husband, he could feel no liking for Emmanuele Vitale but the man commanded respect, a fiery spirit planning a campaign that as far as Peard could see had little chance of success. But neither Julia nor Vitale occupied his thoughts for long, for he was worried about his ship.

Twenty-five years in the Navy and a thousand chances and hazards of war had made Shuldham Peard all but indifferent to personal danger. The placid good-humour of his expression under fire was not a mask but the reflection of a settled confidence, an imperturbability hard won in a quarter-century of war with the French, the Spaniards, the rebel colonists of America, and the merciless sea. Anxiety for himself, with (as he believed) the lusts and melancholies of youth, was an emotion of the past, but *Success* was a different matter and he was anxious about her now. Vitale had said that the French made no patrols but Vitale could be wrong. Sunrise, in an hour or two now, would find the frigate conspicuous and embayed a mere couple of leagues from the harbour that sheltered *Diane* and the other enemy ships – no doubt there were cutters and brigs there too.

In General Vaubois's place, Peard would have had a cutter patrolling the coast every few days. And surely sea communication was kept up with the garrison on Gozo, only four miles to the north-west of Malta island? A supply vessel sailing from Valletta for Gozo would pass Salina Bay keeping no more than three miles offshore to round Amrax Point. And *Success* would have to stay on this coast for days, perhaps weeks, vulnerable to bombardment from the sea and – if Vaubois discovered him – to artillery on the cliffs above the bay.

These increasingly disquieting matters filled his mind while the *carrozza* rocked across the dark countryside and the little steward, huddled in a corner, dutifully held his tongue until such time as his captain chose to address him. By the time the carriage drew up at the point where the path to the bay left the track, Peard was almost ready to believe that some disaster could have overtaken his frigate in his absence.

He sprang down and made, through Boney, an urgent request to Kazan: the 'chief man of Bugibba' would please see to it that only those fishermen who normally worked from Salina Bay came near it – no women or children or idlers. Kazan nodded assurance, waved aside the gold coin Peard offered, and trundled away down the hill. With the steward at his heels Peard scrambled down the precipitous path, twice almost coming to grief through disregarding his footing in order to look for the frigate. A film of cloud was fast obscuring the stars and she was invisible. Down on the shingle, Boney produced a blue-light from his satchel and Peard struck flint and steel to ignite it. Within thirty seconds the answering star flared across half-a-mile of black water and he could spare an inward grin for his exaggerated fears. The wind was veering southerly, he was sure, a fair wind should he wish to sail her clear; and plans for her safety already half-formed would take more definite shape when he'd had an hour or two's sleep.

But not until the cutter had grounded on the shingle and Tildesley had assured him that all was well on board, not until he was in the sternsheets with the boat heading back to *Success*, did Peard find room in his thoughts for things other than his frigate. Then he found himself picturing the candle-lit room, dark-brown tresses framing a face of bewitching loveliness, the white curve of breasts revealed when she curtseyed to him. By God, she was a beauty in a thousand! Had a kindness for him, too, if liquid brown eyes could speak the truth – an angry mental effort dismissed Julia and her charms. He remembered Lucy's last letter, begging him to run into no unnecessary danger. The sooner he sailed away from Malta, Captain Peard told himself, the better.

2

'Like a bloody 'en with one bloody chick,' said Boyce, able
seaman, lifting a lump of sand on his toes and tossing it into
the sea. 'Warp 'er 'ere, tow 'er there, out to the point to look at
'er an' back for another dose. Gaw!'
He spat tobacco-juice between his outstretched feet.
Sheehy, his crony and fellow-member of Number Seven gun-
crew, looked up from the design he was making with white
pebbles.
'By damn, Jack, you'd do the same if 'twas but the one
chick ye had,' he said. 'Where's all of us if the Frinch get a
blink o' the eye at the old *Success*?'
The two were lying on a narrow sunlit crescent of beach
close under the cliffs of Salina Bay in company with some
three dozen others of the frigate's crew, constituting one-half
of the watch-below. At either end of the beach, where the cliffs
sent down tumbled rocks to enclose it, stood a marine sentry.
Success was not to be seen from the beach, but a constant
hammering and buzz of voices from beyond the seaward
corner indicated her presence.
' 'Tis in me mind, Jack,' continued Sheehy, 'that another
cap'n might ha' let us suffer drouth the while he held on for
Alexandria. Sure and he's wine enough aft for himself. Praise
the saints the water's coming aboard tomorrow!' He smacked
his lips. 'I declare to ye I'm that dry I'd drink a mug of – '
'Aw, stuff it!' Boyce scrambled to his feet. 'Come on in an'
wet y'self.'
Mother-naked and hairy, they flung themselves into the
tepid water.
Yesterday there had been little respite for any of the 190
officers and men of the frigate's complement. At first light
Peard (having had two hours' sleep after his run ashore) had
set cutter, longboat and gig to work sounding in the bay
according to his directions. While this was going on Jacques

and his marines were investigating the ruined towers and their approaches; Mr Shorrocks the gunner and Mr Broster the boatswain, with their respective parties of sweating seamen, were casting-loose and preparing two of the after 12-pounders, packing powder and shot, and laying out hawsers and tackles under the supervision of the third lieutenant; and Wrench with half-a-dozen topmen was exploring the cliff-faces in search of reasonable routes of ascent. In the midst of all the activity the five lateen-rigged boats which constituted Bugibba's fishing fleet had put to sea on their daily task, their occupants waving a cheerful greeting to the frigate and her boats. Peard was relieved to see that Hannibal Kazan had kept his word; there were no curious onlookers from the village on the inlet beach or the cliffs.

The alternative plan that had crossed his mind – that of taking *Success* out of the bay and standing off-and-on – had been dismissed. It would give him the chance to fight or manoeuvre, even to run for it, if the French sent a vessel along the coast. But two things were against it: first, he needed to be ready to take water and spars aboard, and secondly putting to sea would make his presence more conspicuous from the coast. The chart and a ruler had shown him that only four miles out from Ras Il-Qawra, the northern headland, he would be in sight from the lofty Valletta fortresses. He would have to conceal the frigate within the bay, as best he could.

With Macaulay and Fossett assisting he transferred to the chart the soundings brought in by the boats. The 3-fathom line ran across the bay halfway in, but there were two possible places where *Success* could lie not far outside this limit, the likeliest in the bight below the curve of the northerly headland. He had her towed into position here, then sailed out of the bay in the cutter to get a view from seaward which showed her all too obvious from any passing craft; towed and warped her to the second alternative, in a narrow deep below the tower on the southern headland, and again put out in the cutter.

This time he was satisfied. The frigate was laid in close to the rocks, fenders rigged, both anchors out, mooring warps secured. Topgallant masts and yards came down to reduce still further the chance of observation, and a shore gangway – no problem in the tideless Mediterranean – constructed. The cliffs on this side, Ras Il-Challis, were no more than fifty or sixty feet high, but even so the next operation, swaying up a 12-pounder to the cliff-top, demanded long preparation and careful execution. By the time it was done darkness had fallen.

That had been Saturday. The customary Sunday-morning ritual of captain's inspection and the reading of the Articles of War went by the board and more work took its place, all hands turning-to for the transport and installation of a second 12-pounder on Ras Il-Qawra and the construction of rock emplacements for both guns. But by noon the jobs were done and able seamen Boyce and Sheehy and their mates could enjoy – in relays – a brief relaxation ashore.

Peard, too, could relax. The situation of the frigate was still dangerous but he had done what he could to render it less so. The lookouts on both headlands, the marines guarding the shore approaches to the bay, the guns commanding the entrance from both sides, could not (he knew) save him if Vaubois got wind of his presence and sent a thousand men by land and *Diane* to blockade him in the bay; but at least they wouldn't catch him napping. Nor was he beset by the worry that would normally affect any captain with his ship moored within jumping-distance of the shore. Apart from the fact that the Successes liked their ship and their captain, it was unlikely that anyone would choose to desert on an island 17 miles long by 9 miles wide, in the hands of the French.

All the same, he could take no risks. Bugibba was just over the headland, and he knew from Boney that there were other villages – Gharghur and Naxxar and Mosta – within a mile or two. And in all these villages were women. So there were marine sentries on the strip of beach selected for recreation and on the shingle of the inlet where the path started up, as well as those patrolling the cliffs. Newly-pressed landsmen might resent having an armed sentry put over them but the hardened seamen who made up threequarters of his crew accepted it as an everyday matter, part of naval routine.

The sole member of the ship's company to be allowed into Bugibba was the captain's steward, and it was Boney who brought the news that the promised water would be carried down to the Salina inlet at first light on Monday. Peard was there with longboat and cutter when the long caravan of laden beasts and men came slithering down the steep path, dark shapes under the paling sky of early morning. As seamen and Maltese worked together to secure the miscellaneous collection of barrels and casks to lines so that they could be towed to the frigate, Boney – who had come with Peard as interpreter – held excited conversation with his uncle.

'Sir – sir!' The steward's voice as he turned to Peard was a joyful screech. 'News, sir, very grand news! The soldiers in Mdina are all killed – all, to the every man jack, sir!'

Sharp questioning elicited some details. It appeared that an indeterminate number of Maltese, led by one Vicenzo Borg, had got inside the walls of the ancient capital after nightfall on Sunday. They had knifed the sentries and entered the military quarters without any alarm given. According to Boney, not a single Frenchman had escaped the massacre that followed. And now, ended the delighted steward, the Maltese 'army' possessed five hundred muskets and large amounts of powder and shot, besides the cannon which had defended the city of Mdina.

Peard felt slightly sick as he listened. War was his trade, but this butchery of unarmed men asleep or half-awake was different from the slaughter that took place, say, when one vessel boarded another, when the enemy could fight back or cry for quarter. No doubt this bloody business was Emmanuele Vitale's 'deed' that was to be done, as he had said, in two days' time. Then he recollected that the massacre at Mdina was the desperate blow of a weak and unarmed people at the far more powerful invaders that had trodden them underfoot. What else could they do if they were resolved to fight? And certainly the thing must have been very well planned. It smacked of Vitale's cold efficiency – but had the Viconde considered the possible sequel? If Vaubois decided to launch his army in a sweep of the island by way of revenge, *Success* would be in immediate danger of discovery.

'A most successful blow indeed,' he said; there was no point in saying more to Boney. 'Now – ask your uncle how much water he has brought us, and how much I am to pay.'

A hundred and twenty *cafisos*; that was something over 450 gallons – he could have wished for more but this was adequate. Kazan would name no sum for payment but seemed well satisfied with the little bag of half-sovereigns Peard handed over for distribution among the water-carriers. It was the captain's insistence on shaking hands, however, that brought a delighted grin to his bearded face, and as Peard turned away he felt his heart warm once again towards the people of Malta. Whether their ancestors were Phoenician or Arabian, their characteristics were more like those of his own countrymen than any Mediterranean race, and this (to his thoroughly British mind) made them doubly worth saving from the French. The promise he had made to Emmanuele Vitale should be kept at the very earliest opportunity.

By now the indispensable water was on its way to the frigate. The surface of the bay was shimmering mother-o'-pearl between the headlands, Ras Il-Challis cliffs night-shadowed still but those of Il-Qawra on the left glowing pink with the first colours of coming day. Across the iridescent sea crept cutter and longboat, each with its long tail of casks, just awash, bobbing astern. A little breeze was beginning to ruffle the pearly water as Peard went down to his gig and he noted with satisfaction that it still blew from the south-west, a fair wind if he had make a dash for the open sea; today's task, once the water was aboard and stowed, would be to see that everything was on a split yarn for that eventuality. The thought did cross his mind that if the French issued forth to take their revenge it might go hard with Emmanuele Vitale's wife, should they find her, but he could spare no anxiety for Julia when his ship was threatened. As soon as he was back on board he summoned Fossett to his cabin, and to the sound of shrieking blocks and thudding casks as the water was swayed up and stored they devised plans for the further safety of *Success*.

For three days nothing happened in or near Salina Bay. The posting and relieving of extra lookouts and sentries, the repeated drill designed to get the frigate out from her hiding-place in the least possible time, settled into a routine with the daily deck-swabbing, shore parties for recreation, and meal-times. Food stores were ample – a frigate could carry provisions for six months – and though Peard would have liked to buy fresh fish from the Maltese fishermen he abstained when he heard what Boney had to tell him. Though the islanders had managed to save some of their possessions from the ravages of the French, hiding grain and beasts in the innumerable caves that honeycombed the limestone hills and cliffs, they were going to be very short of food in the coming winter.

Instead he encouraged his men to fish in the off-duty periods, thereby causing O'Halloran the cook to make some disastrous experiments in the boiling of cuttlefish and sea-urchins. On the third day he learned from Boney, his one source of information about events on the island, that a column of French soldiers had marched out of Valletta on the day following the slaughter at Mdina; the Maltese, forewarned, had laid an ambush and wrought such havoc with their captured muskets that the French had hastily retreated behind their walls again.

For the first time Peard gave some thought to the strategic aspect of the Malta situation. Obviously no amount of skirmishing with muskets could ever dislodge Vaubois and his 4,000 men from fortified Valletta, but it was beginning to look as if they could be penned there from the landward side. Through Boney, who relayed the information given him by Hannibal Kazan, he had learned that a Committee of Three had been formed to organise the Maltese resistance, composed of Vicenzo Borg who had led the Mdina attack, Emmanuele

Vitale, and Canon Caruana, a churchman. A system of messengers to connect the scattered *casals* had been arranged and every man capable of bearing arms was to be in readiness to muster; Kazan himself was a sergeant in this irregular militia.

Here was an ordered determination that could perhaps ensure that landward blockade, but while Valletta could be supplied by sea – and De Brueys's fleet, when it returned, would see to that – Vaubois could maintain his position. If only a British fleet could sail to blockade Valletta! Peard remembered that magnificent harbour, spacious, deep water everywhere, impregnable to assault, now a legitimate objective of war, and saw it in British hands – the Mediterranean naval base of the future. If French ambitions moved eastward, towards India, it would be invaluable. His impatience to leave Malta grew.

The sixth day of September dawned still and breathless. Two days ago the faint sou'-westerly airs had fallen away, leaving a dead calm with such drift of air as there was coming from the north. There had been no word from Vitale, and despite his habitual equanimity Peard was getting anxious about the promised spars. Halfway through the forenoon watch he had himself pulled ashore in the gig, landing at the inlet. The marine sentries at the foot and the top of the little path saluted as he passed them, to turn left and walk along the cliff edge with the still waters of the bay shimmering below and the rugged landscape on his right dancing in the heat-haze.

After a word with the lookouts on the Challis headland he retraced his steps as far as the promontory above the salt-pans and then diverged to mount a stony hillock that gave a view to the south-east. Beyond two miles of broken ground, rock and dry watercourse diversified by tiny patches of cultivation, the pale crags of the Gharghur ridge hoisted their long rank of buttress and cleft. Vitale's house of Tal-Marfa must be hidden among the chaos of giant boulders at their feet; small wonder that it had escaped the ravages of the invaders. He could see much nearer at hand the faint line of the unfenced track by which the *carrozza* had taken him to Tal-Marfa; and as he looked two riders emerged into sight from a dip in the track half-a-mile away, trotting their mounts towards the Salina Bay inlet.

Peard came down from his hillock with long strides to intercept them. Even at that distance he could make out that one of the riders was a woman, and he was irritably conscious of a small but definite excitement at the thought that it might be Julia Vitale. They saw him, and reined-in at the junction of the inlet path with the track, a hundred yards from the marine sentry who had advanced his musket and was preparing to challenge them. As Peard approached the woman gestured imperiously to the man who sat his horse behind her and he sprang down to help her dismount. It was Julia. She walked quickly to meet him, holding the skirts of her dark-blue riding-habit clear of the dusty ground.

'Ma'am, your most obedient.' Peard made his bow as they met. 'This is an unexpected – '

'*Parlons français, m'sieu,*' she cut him short; and then in quaint English, with a smile, 'We did speak French together as – children, am I not right?'

A little hat with a feather in it was perched on the shining coils of her hair. The blue tunic that clung so closely to her magnificent figure had a white frill at neck and bosom. He found himself staring and removed his gaze abruptly.

'My French is at your service, madame,' he replied in that language. 'Though it is less –'

'Less suited to business than to – *l'amour?*' Julia laughed, her brown eyes sparkling wickedly. 'But forgive me, monsieur,' she added swiftly. 'I am the bearer of a message from my husband.' She took a sealed letter from the flapped pocket of her habit and gave it to him. 'I believe it is urgent.'

Peard paused with a finger on the seal, frowning. 'Monsieur Vitale sent you with this? Surely there is still some danger that the French may send out patrols?'

She shrugged. 'You must have heard how the brave Maltese dealt with their last attempt to come out.' There was a touch of contempt in her tone. 'And I am not to be "sent", monsieur, by any man. Emmanuele told Mattei to bring it. I took it from him and bade him ride with me – I wished to see you again,' she ended frankly.

He was very conscious of her nearness and the warmth of her gaze as she looked up at him under long dark lashes. But Vitale's letter was in his hands.

'Permit me, madame,' he said firmly, breaking the seal.

There were two short paragraphs in an angular hand, without preamble or signature:

We have the spars. They will reach you tonight by fishing-vessel from Balluta.

Peard gave a grunt of intense satisfaction. His eyes widened as he read the second paragraph.

There is news from inside Valletta. The Guillaume Tell *was damaged in a great battle with your ships on the first day of August, in Aboukir Bay. I can tell you no more, except that it is believed the victory was to the British.*

Aboukir – that was three leagues from Alexandria. And seven weeks ago. Nelson must have found De Brueys, then, and *a great battle* meant that two dozen or more ships of the line had engaged. He would almost have given those precious spars for more news. How had the English ships fared? He knew them all and most of their captains, in particular Ball, captain of *Alexander*, who was an old friend. But he had no doubt of the victory. Nelson would make sure of that. Controlling his inner excitement, he looked up to thank Vitale's messenger and found that she had moved away to seat herself on a flat-topped rock. She had taken off the feathered hat and was fanning herself with it.

'There was good news in your letter, I believe,' she said as Peard came to her. 'Emmanuele told me of it.'

'Yes. Good news for me and for Malta. My thanks to you,

madame, for bringing it.'

'For Malta,' she repeated slowly. 'You think so?'

He glanced at her in surprise. 'Certainly. That is, if the French fleet is gravely damaged. In that case Vaubois can no longer count upon support by sea and Valletta must surrender to a British fleet.'

'*C'est entendu.* Monsieur, pray sit down,' Julia patted the rock beside her. 'It is not intolerable here, I assure you,' she added impishly as he hesitated.

Peard sat down gingerly all the same, for he was wearing his thinnest pair of white breeches and by noon on a day like this the rocks of Malta would be too hot to touch. The rock was not a big one and Julia's dark-blue skirt brushed against his knee.

'It was not "monsieur" and "madame" with us all those years ago, Peard,' she murmured with a sidelong glance. 'I called you "Peard" then – you remember?'

'Yes,' he said uncomfortably.

'*Un gros mensonge, je crois.* I have never forgotten, Peard. But –' her voice changed – 'you shall answer a question for me. Suppose Valletta is surrendered and the British become lords of Malta. Will they return the island to the Knights of St John?'

Peard, relieved by this change of subject, rubbed his chin and considered. His vision of Malta as a British naval base would hardly accord with the renewal of a seignory with a Grand Master at its head.

'I cannot answer for the government of my country, madame,' he replied cautiously. 'For my part, I would support the cause your husband is working for. The Maltese – '

'Emmanuele?' She spat out the name with infinite scorn. 'You would support him – a Jacobin, a mob-raiser? For that is what he is, as much as those *sales bêtes* in Paris!'

'I would support the idea that the people of Malta should govern their own island.'

'*Dieu-de-dieu!*' Julia turned on him angrily. 'It is not theirs!

It was given to us – to the Knights Hospitallers – three
hundred years ago. It belongs to us still. Emmanuele may
have betrayed his Order but I – I am still a Boisredin, Peard!'

'It seems I must beg your pardon,' he said, frowning. 'I was
not aware that you – '

'No – you are ignorant, Monsieur Peard. The French know
our history better than you. If they keep Malta they will
reinstate the Knights. This I have been told by one of them.'

'Perhaps by General Bonaparte?' said Peard, stung into
sarcasm. 'Naturally he has begun the reinstatement by
shipping most of your Knights off to Sicily and stealing their
treasure.'

Julia snapped her fingers. 'Bah – what is he? A mere
general, not even a Frenchman. An ignorant Corsican who
has as little knowledge of our history as you. He no more
represents France than does his precious army – the scum of
Italy and Venice and half Europe. The French navy is
different. Half the officers are Royalists and only wait their
time to get rid of *parvenus* like Bonaparte.'

Peard stared, half inclined to laugh. 'Who told you that,
madame?'

'A French sea officer of your own rank,' she answered with a
defiant toss of her head. 'His ship was damaged in a March
grigal and put into Valletta for repairs. My father entertained
him for a week and I had much talk with Captain Jean-
Gagneraud.'

Peard started and frowned at the name and Julia,
misinterpreting his reaction, laughed and laid a hand on his
knee.

'You need not be jealous, *mon ami*,' she told him. 'Though
indeed – ' she regarded him critically – 'Gagneraud is much
better looking than you and has far better manners. And at
least he could tell me positively that France would be bound in
honour to maintain the Knights as rulers of Malta.'

'I think you would find that Captain Gagneraud is
mistaken,' said Peard.

The sun was at its zenith and the sweat was trickling down

his spine. The red coat and white crossbelts of a marine appeared coming up to relieve the sentry at the top of the inlet path, and as the spot of bright colour caught his eye the sound of eight bells being struck on board the invisible *Success* came clearly on the hot still air. He stood up.

'I must go,' he said abruptly. 'My thanks, madame, for – '

'Your hand, monsieur, if you please,' Julia commanded.

With a muttered apology he helped her to her feet. The movement brought them breast to breast and she retained her grasp of his hand.

'Peard,' she murmured, looking up at him, 'we have wasted so much time talking politics. We must meet again. You will not sail until tomorrow?'

'Tomorrow night. But I – '

'Listen. There is a place not far from here, a ruin – an ancient temple, perhaps of Venus.' The low-voiced words came faster. 'We will meet there tonight. The moon is full – I will send Mattei here at midnight with a horse for you. You have not forgotten – that first time?'

She was pressed close to him, her fragrance in his nostrils, her red lips tempting him.

'It is long ago,' he muttered. 'We were very young, Julia.'

'*Tiens*, here is gallantry!' she said lightly, but the brown eyes were avid. 'May we not renew our youth, then? Peard – you'll come?'

The urge of temptation was undeniable and it angered him. No doubt the Shuldham Peard of twenty years ago would have yielded without a thought, but facing her now was a thirty-seven-year-old man long accustomed to confronting his impulses with their probable consequences; a man who prided himself on an inviolable loyalty and who had given that loyalty to his Service and – three years ago – to Lucy.

'I am sensible of the honour, madame,' he said coldly. 'But I shall not come.'

Julia snatched her hand away and stepped back, her eyes aflame. For a moment he thought she would strike him.

'My duty, as of course you realise,' he went on, 'requires me to be on board my ship.'

Her gaze was steady on him, and the distortion of rage suddenly gave place to a little smile.

'*Soit*,' she said in a tone as even as his own. 'But you will come back to Malta, Peard. We shall meet again.'

Without another word she turned and walked quickly to where the groom waited with the horses. Peard watched her mount and ride away, never turning her head to look back, with the man cantering behind her. Then he let out his breath in a long, voluminous sigh. It was almost entirely a sigh of relief; but it held, perhaps, just a touch of nostalgia for vanished youth.

3

A persistent calm hung over the southern Mediterranean. Day after day the wide blue circle of the sea lay motionless round the frigate, with no wind except for an occasional feeble puff from the north to move her limp sails. Hoisting every scrap of canvas she could wear, hauling and slackening to catch every breath of air, Peard had managed in three days to sink the coast of Malta astern; but even now from the masthead the turreted dome of Mdina cathedral could be seen notching the southern horizon. Any westward progress had been prevented by the easterly-setting current along the Cyrenaican coast.

The promised spars had duly arrived on board *Success*, brought by a big felucca in the early hours of the morning, and at nightfall of that day the frigate had put to sea with her new mizen yard and fore topgallant mast in position. They had had to tow her out from Salina Bay, and when the boats were back on board it was only by grace of light airs, the ghost of a land-breeze off the island, that she had gained six miles away from the coast by sunrise. The news of a battle a month ago had impelled Peard to head westward, back to Gibraltar. Nelson would certainly not linger in the eastern Mediterranean but would return to his base, and it was probable that he had already completed the 2,000-mile voyage from Alexandria to the Rock. But with no wind fair or foul to move her *Success* could do nothing to implement her captain's decision. The urgency of Malta's need for aid grew upon Peard with every watch, straining his habitual patience to its limit; and when young Mr Tildesley (a Classical scholar) ventured to remark that at least they were adhering to Caesar Augustus's motto of *festina lente*, he received a glare that caused him to revise his conviction of his captain's unvarying good-humour.

At two bells of the afternoon watch, with *Success* trying to pick up the increasing puffs that made catspaws on the waveless sea, the masthead hailed to report a fleet of big ships, a dozen at least, on the larboard bow. Peard, at the crosstrees with his telescope, made out thirteen 74's, nearly all of them showing – even at a distance – the tattered canvas and lack of spars that must be the results of battle. As the frigate crawled slowly towards them with the lightest of breezes now developing to help her he saw that one of them, with sails riddled but masts intact, wore British colours and a broad pendant; and he was soon able to identify her as *Orion*, 74, commanded by Sir James Saumarez who was Nelson's second-in-command.

Ninety minutes later (for even his cutter full-rigged could do no better with that fitful breeze) Peard was seated in *Orion*'s stern-cabin making his report to the senior captain. Signs of makeshift repair were all about him: great holes plugged in the bulkhead, smashed windows boarded over, the scrubbed planking of the deck grooved in half-a-dozen places where the half-spent balls had driven across. Saumarez himself had shared the battering his ship had taken, for he sat at his table with one bandage-swathed leg resting on a padded stool and his upper body was bulky with bandaging beneath his blue coat. Peard knew better than to comment or question, however; Sir James had a short way with babblers for all his habitual courtesy. He reported his doings and findings as briefly as he could while Saumarez, his pale saturnine face expressionless, heard him out.

'Very well,' he said, when Peard had ended with his own opinion that help should be sent to Malta. 'You'll understand I can do little at this moment. I've *Orion* and a dozen patched-up seventy-fours to get to Gibraltar, seven of them French prizes, and I wouldn't be this close to Malta if it wasn't for this damned calm and the southerly drift. What's more, there's a breeze springing up at last and I can't delay. You say the Maltese are organising themselves against the French?'

'And to some effect, Sir James. Their immediate need is for arms.'

'I can do something to remedy that.' Saumarez drew pen and paper towards him and began to write. 'Twelve hundred captured muskets, with all available powder and shot. Foley has them in *Goliath*. I'll have them sent ashore to – what's the place? – Salina Bay. I take it this man Kazan may safely receive them?'

'Certainly. With the wind holding,' Peard added, '*Success* could take them in.'

'I believe your orders require you to join the Admiral, Captain Peard,' Saumarez said drily. 'Sir Horatio is at Naples with *Vanguard* and four of the line. This news of Malta should be conveyed to him immediately. Nelson was wounded, by the bye, though not severely.'

'I'm sorry to hear that.' Peard could contain his eagerness for news no longer. 'But the battle at Aboukir, Sir James – I've heard nothing except that we gained the victory. Will you – '

'We smashed De Brueys,' Saumarez cut him short. 'Of his thirteen ships nine were taken and two burnt. For the rest of the tale I'll refer you to Cutler, my first lieutenant. I've much to do.'

He glanced up at the telltale compass in the deckhead as *Orion* very slowly shifted her massive hull with the rising breeze, and considered for a moment, frowning. Then he spoke briskly.

'I shall send a flag of truce in to Valletta demanding the surrender of the French. I can do no less, and – alas! – no more. You'll please to wait on board, sir, until Vaubois's reply is received. Cutler will entertain you.' He raised his voice. 'Mr Trelawney!'

A lanky midshipman, appearing from nowhere, escorted Peard out onto the after-deck, where parties of seamen were busy overhauling cordage and painting newly-repaired sections of the rail. The light northerly breeze had steadied and *Success* had come up to lie half-a-mile to leeward of the squadron of crippled warships. Mr Cutler, discovered in his cabin checking store-lists with the purser, proved to be a cheerful round-faced man whose skull was almost hidden under strips of sticking-plaster (a musket-shot from *Aquilon*'s maintop, he told Peard) and whose hospitality extended to a bottle of excellent madeira.

Dismissing the purser with a sigh of relief, he poured two glasses while his guest briefly explained his presence on board *Orion*. And now at last Peard heard a first-hand account of the battle of the Nile: of Nelson's daring attack inshore of the anchored French line; of the ten-hour fight, broadside after broadside at close range; of the tremendous explosion when *L'Orient*, De Brueys's 120-gun flagship, blew up and sank with all hands.

'*Alexander* was pounding her when she caught fire,' said Cutler. 'Ball drenched his sails with water and kept his station to make sure of her.'

It was a tale long in the telling, necessitating the use of books and every other small article in the cabin to illustrate the tactics of the attacking ships. The hours flew by, the madeira sank in the bottle. Peard and Cutler were on hands and knees on the cabin deck, Cutler whisking away Norie's *Seamanship* and an empty glass to represent the flight of *Guillaume Tell* and *Généreux*, when a midshipman banged on the door and stuck his head in: Mr Brett's compliments and the cutter was in sight, returning from Valletta. In half-an-hour she had come alongside and delivered her news. Captain Peard's presence was requested in the stern-cabin.

'Vaubois declined to surrender,' Saumarez told him. 'Not

an instant's hesitation. That was to be expected, of course – Valletta can never be taken from the sea.' He handed over a folded paper. 'You'll carry my report to the Admiral. You'll be in Naples a week or more before I reach Gib.'

'I wish you a fair wind, Sir James,' said Peard, preparing to depart.

'One moment,' said Saumarez; he paused, frowning and rubbing his injured leg. 'You hinted that you'd ask the Admiral to send help to Malta as soon as possible. You said, I fancy, that he would see the vast importance of obtaining Valletta for our Mediterranean base. I must tell you, Peard, that Nelson won't see that – he's never had any opinion of Malta. He wants to base the Fleet on Naples.'

'But – there is in fact no comparison,' Peard said, raising his brows. 'For defensibility Valletta's by far the – '

'Sir Horatio has – friends in Naples,' Saumarez interrupted flatly. 'They weigh more with him than defensibility. Let me add that in this matter I'm wholly on your side, as any sea-officer would be who – ' He checked himself and fingered his chin reflectively. 'Do you know Ball of the *Alexander*?'

'We're old friends, Sir James.'

'See Ball as soon as you get ashore. Nelson will always listen to Ball. You'll remember last May off Cape Sicié, no doubt.'

Peard nodded. It was the daring seamanship of Alexander Ball that had saved the dismasted *Vanguard* from running on the rocks of Cape Sicié; had saved Nelson's life, in all probability.

'You'll have Ball's backing, depend upon it,' added Saumarez.

From outside the cabin door came the click of heels as the marine sentry jumped to attention, and the first lieutenant came in.

'*Goliath*'s cutter has returned, sir, and she's signalling – "mission completed".'

'Very well, Mr Cutler. Signal the squadron "make sail".' Saumarez turned to Peard. 'There's your muskets delivered – let's hope they make good use of them. And good fortune attend you at Naples, Captain Peard.'

'Thank you, Sir James. It sounds as though I may need it.'

From the sternsheets of the frigate's cutter Peard looked back across the widening space of wind-rippled blue to Saumarez's squadron of cripples, now slowly forming line. *Tonnant, Aquilon, Franklin, Conquérant, Peuple-Souverain* – rags of canvas on stumps of masts, the great ships that had been the pride of the French Navy were a pitiable sight. The victory they betokened could be a major turning-point in the long war with France, more significant by far than the fate of Malta. Yet it was Malta that bulked more largely in his thoughts. Peard grinned, a trifle ruefully, as he considered his new rôle. In place of the zealous captain intent on placing himself under his Admiral's command there was now, it seemed, a zealous missionary seeking to convert that Admiral to his own faith.

As he came on board *Success* to the squeal of bosun's pipes he was aware that every officer and man on deck was staring at him in a peculiar way. For an instant he thought the hospitable Cutler's madeira might have led him to omit the fastening of essential buttons, and darted an anxious glance at his immaculate breeches. Then he realised that they were all thirsting for news, for the explanation of the ruinous squadron under their lee. Well, he was not a town crier and they could wait. He would invite the wardroom officers to dine with him; what was said aft, in a floating wooden box 130 feet long by 30 feet wide, would be retailed for'ard within minutes.

'Very well, Mr Fossett,' he said, returning the first lieutenant's salute. 'We may make sail as soon as the cutter's inboard. Mr Macauley, I'll thank you to lay a course for Naples.'

CHAPTER THREE

Calypso

1

The steadying northerly, a foul wind for the Messina strait but fair for west-about Sicily, gave *Success* a good run for 200 sea-miles. The levanter she had hoped to pick up when she had cleared the Egadi islands did not materialize, however, and a fitful north-easter kept her beating back and forth on her course to Naples; much to the annoyance of her crew, who were eagerly looking forward to their long-delayed run ashore.

Her captain had other reasons for impatience. The predicament of the Maltese, planning a campaign against a foe of overwhelming strength, gave him increasing anxiety, and the notion of securing Valletta as a naval base grew upon him. The destruction of their Mediterranean fleet did not mean that the French would abandon an army of 4,000 men on Malta; sooner or later they would attempt to relieve them and establish Valletta firmly in French hands. And there was a more imminent possibility: General Vaubois might bestir himself and deploy his troops for a thorough sweep of the island, annihilating all resistance – and, perhaps, the Maltese race itself.

Help they must have and speedily, Peard told himself, pacing his quarterdeck under the windy stars. Ships must be found for a blockade, troops and guns landed in force to assault Valletta from landward. Vitale and his associates were not soldiers, nor were a few hundred muskets the armament for a long siege however enthusiastically they were handled.

Recollection of Vitale brought Julia into Peard's mind. He had scarcely thought of her during the past few days and now she stood clearly in his remembrance, pictured in that moment on the cliffs above Salina Bay before she had turned to ride away. It was a moment, he realised, that had added something like respect to the physical attraction he felt when she was near him. She had offered herself and his refusal must have been like a blow in the face; yet she had kept her dignity, had even smiled – he could see the curve of the full red lips now. He could admire that, for it showed the sort of spirit he valued. The possibility that he might see Julia again before very long was not at all unpleasant.

Julia Vitale had no further place in Peard's thoughts once the cone of Vesuvius was sighted on the northern horizon. On a hazy September morning *Success* crept into the Gulf and found anchorage on the outskirts of the mass of shipping that lay along the quays below the tiered pink and white houses of the town, with the fetid stink of the waterfront alleys (remembered of old by her captain) replacing the clean salt air of the past weeks.

Nothing was to be seen of *Vanguard* or of an admiral's flag among the forest of masts, but the massive hull of the *Alexander* was there, her command pendant flapping listlessly at the main, and before the frigate had rounded to her anchor a signal-hoist ran up to the yardarm of the 74. Midshipman Hepplewhite spelled it out with the aid of his telescope.

'A-V-E – "ave successus", sir,' he piped in puzzled tones, glancing apprehensively at the captain.

'Quite correct, Mr Hepplewhite,' said Peard. 'It's Latin. But I fancy you've not read all of it.'

Mr Hepplewhite blushed. 'Oh – er – "captain come on board", sir.'

'Pass the word for my coxswain. Mr Fossett, please see that those craft keep a good four fathoms clear.' Peard pointed to the approaching flotilla of bum-boats and sample-craft from the brothels. 'I'm going on board *Alexander*.'

He was smiling inwardly as the gig gathered way through

the crowd of shore-boats, remembering the gunroom of
Ramillies twenty-five years ago and Alex Ball's whim of
addressing his juniors in dog-Latin. Ball had been senior mid,
Peard newly-joined and five years younger, but their
friendship had survived separation into different ships and the
infrequency of their meetings. He had last encountered Ball
two years ago in Syracuse, covered in white dust and directing
a blaspheming party of seamen in the excavation of an ancient
Greek portico; Alex had recently developed an enthusiasm for
the bygone civilisations of the Mediterranean and with him
enthusiasm meant dedication.

There were neatly-plugged shot-holes in *Alexander*'s side
and most of her larboard rail looked new, but the spotless
after-deck to which Peard climbed showed no sign of the fierce
battle of seven weeks ago. Captain Ball, in the presence of
white-gloved sideboys and marines presenting arms, received
his visitor formally, his long face dour and expressionless.
Once in the privacy of his day-cabin, however, he tossed his
hat into a corner, shouted for his steward, and gripped Peard's
shoulders.

'Young Shuldham, by Jupiter!' he exclaimed in his high,
oddly boyish voice. 'Go hang yourself – we fought at Aboukir,
and you were not there. What fortunate wind brings you to
Naples?'

He was as tall as Peard but slim and elegant in contrast
with his friend's sturdy breadth. Below a very high forehead
two singularly penetrating grey eyes, normally hard and cold,
were sparkling now with pleasure as he surveyed Peard. The
entrance of the steward bearing wine and glasses broke in on
the frigate captain's explanation of his presence.

'A wine of Marsala,' said Ball, pouring it. 'Not your true
Falernian but 'twill serve. To your future, *amicus meus*,
wherever it leads you.'

'It leads me to the Admiral as soon as I can find him,' Peard
said, setting down his glass. 'I looked for *Vanguard* as I came in
but couldn't see her.'

'*Vanguard*'s in Castellmare dockyard, and never did a

seventy-four need a dockyard more. As for Nelson – ' Ball paused and a shadow flitted across his long countenance – 'Nelson's recovering from his wound, ashore in the Sessa palace. He's deputed Hardy – that's big Tom Hardy, who's his flag-captain now – to act for him in everything. Hardy's in Castellamare on board *Vanguard*.'

'I fancy my report – I have it with me – should go to the Admiral himself. In my opinion, Alex, it's a matter to be dealt with by Nelson, and at once. It concerns the situation on Malta.'

Ball looked up sharply from pouring a second glass. 'Malta? The Melita of the Greeks. You've been ashore there? Did you come upon any ancient ruins?'

'I – er – heard of a ruined temple.' Peard firmly dismissed the vision of Julia his words invoked. 'But I believe it was to Venus, and she was Roman.'

'Indeed she was! And the Romans were in Malta some nineteen centuries ago, after – ' Ball stopped himself quickly. 'But the present situation there is the subject of your report.'

'Yes. And Saumarez told me I'd do well to consult you about it. I told you I encountered Sir James and the prizes becalmed off Valletta.'

'You did. And Jamie Saumarez and I see eye-to-eye in most matters, so proceed, young Shuldham, *ab ovo usque ad mala*.'

With this encouragement and that of the Marsala wine, Peard recounted in detail what he had seen and heard in Malta (omitting, however, to mention Julia Vitale) and ended by expressing his own opinion, with a force that surprised himself, that to strike swiftly could win an incomparable naval base for Britain.

'And by Jupiter you're right!' Ball cried, his deepset eyes alive with excitement. 'I've said the same these many years. Valletta commands the Mediterranean both east and west. Mahon and the Rock cramp us up in the western end, and any mainland base – why, see how thoroughly the French army threw us out of Toulon in ninety-three.'

'Yet the Admiral – or so I'm informed – envisages Naples as

our future base,' Peard said cautiously.

'Ye-e-es. But he could be – he might be turned.'

Ball frowned and pinched the tip of his long nose between finger and thumb, his gaze steady on the frigate captain.

'You were ever an oyster for closeness, Shuldham,' he said suddenly. 'Be close about what I say to you now. Nelson's in a trap here, a trap sprung by his own weakness. Don't mistake me – there never was a stronger man in command at sea, as the Nile battle proves. But I've learnt that his strength depends on the approbation of all about him, and therein lies his weakness, too. For, d'you see, it's but a step from that to believing flattery – *viscus merus est blanditia* – and here in Naples he's buttered, swamped, smothered with flattery by every soul from the King of the Two Sicilies downwards. That is,' he added bitterly, 'if there *is* anything lower than Ferdinand.'

'But he's recovered from his wound?' Peard put in.

'Maybe, and maybe not. It was a head wound, d'you see, and that could have something to do with his present shape. Be that as it may, Sir William Hamilton and his lady have got him up there at the Palazzo Sessa, doctors and women fussing over him all day, not to be worried by affairs of the Fleet. Every night for the past ten days he's rigged out in full-dress and hauled here, there and everywhere to fêtes and Court banquets in his honour. That woman seems to think she owns him.'

'Lady Hamilton?'

Ball nodded, tight-lipped. 'Emma Hamilton. Sir William married his concubine five years ago, which makes the British Embassy – very suitably – the only respectable house in Naples. I've heard Nelson himself say it's a city of whores and scoundrels. But let me tell you what's passed since *Vanguard* arrived.'

He told of the hysterical welcome afforded to the Hero of the Nile, five hundred lavishly decorated boats greeting the flagship, Queen Maria Carolina and the British Ambassadress swooning away (Lady Hamilton into Nelson's one arm), fireworks and drunken revelry night after night,

Nelson hailed as 'the Saviour of the World', flags, bunting, illuminations, 'See the Conquering Hero' endlessly resounding from a score of discordant bands.

'And they keep at it,' Ball said exasperatedly. 'Tomorrow night there's another banquet at the Royal Palace, to celebrate Nelson's fortieth birthday. Eighteen hundred guests, Troubridge of the *Culloden* and myself among 'em.' He slapped his thigh. 'That's our chance, by Jupiter! Somehow we'll get him apart in private and lay this matter of Malta before him. God knows what the result will be but we'll do our damnedest. If you'll give that report of yours into my charge – '

'Very willingly.' Peard handed it over. 'I'm grateful, Alex. And, while I think of it, a question for you. Supposing our hopes are realised and Valletta falls to a British attack, would Government hand Malta back to the Knights of St John?'

Ball shook his head. 'What the politicos would do no man can tell. For my part, if I had any say in it I'd take damned good care that the Knights never got their claws into Malta again. There's a dozen of 'em here, refugees, and they fit into Ferdinand's bawdy-house of a Court as snug as pigs fit a sty – I can't say worse than that.' He refilled their glasses. 'The devil take politics. Tell me about *Success*.'

'Not a bit of it. I want to hear about *Alexander* at the Nile. I'm told you did nobly.'

'You may say that of my lads,' Ball said. 'They fought their guns like heroes. Well, now. We came in just astern of *Swiftsure*, d'you see, to find *Bellerophon* drifting clear of *L'Orient* with Darby and a third of her crew killed – '

They fought the Nile again until it was time for Peard to return to his ship.

For the next thirty-six hours the captain of *Success* was uncommonly busy. He did not know what orders he might receive, but it was certain that a frigate, one of the few in service, would not remain in port for long. Of the war situation in the Mediterranean he knew little; but though General Bonaparte's army in Egypt had lost its naval support by the Battle of the Nile there was another French army threatening Naples from the north, and while half the British Mediterranean fleet was disabled the twenty-five French battleships in Brest might get to sea and force their way in past Gibraltar.

Success might be sent east or west, or – and his hopes lay here – south. In any case she must be in every particular ready to sail. So while his crew went ashore by watches, returning drunk and singing, Peard hurried from dockyard to arsenal and from arsenal to warehouse bullying or bribing reluctant Neapolitans into supplying him with stores and ammunition. He could get no help for the frigate's wounded foredeck from the dockyard, where *Vanguard* and *Culloden* occupied the whole labour force with their repairs; instead he connived at a piece of thievery by which Mr Neal the carpenter was enabled to complete, with some prime planking, the repairs begun in Salina Bay. He was inspecting the half-completed job when Wrench, who was duty officer, reported a boat approaching from *Alexander*.

'Sideparty, Mr Wrench, if you please,' said Peard, and hastened aft to receive Captain Ball with due ceremony.

'Well, 'tis done,' said Ball, sitting down in the stern-cabin, 'and with a degree of success. The neatest cutting-out expedition you ever saw.'

He waited until the captain's steward, who had come in with the customary refreshment, had left the cabin.

'That's the man you've mentioned, I take it – Bonici. I'm going to ask you for a temporary loan of Bonici, Shuldham.' He nodded at Peard's quick look of interrogation. 'Yes. We sail for Malta on fourth October, when I'll be hoisting a broad pendant in *Alexander*. Murray in *Colossus*, *Culloden* if she completes in time, *Success* and the *Belle Citoyenne* brig – that's my squadron.'

'And good luck to Commodore Ball,' said Peard, raising his glass. 'But – no troops? No siege-guns?'

'No. We're lucky to get so much, let me tell you. I'd the devil's own job with the Admiral. But he's giving me a Portuguese squadron, two or three ships under the Marquis de Niza, when they come in.' Ball grimaced drolly. 'You have to be a nobleman to captain a Portuguese warship. But no doubt they'll be of use in the blockade. For those are my orders – to maintain a strict blockade of Valletta.'

'Then Vaubois may hold out for a year or more,' Peard frowned. 'But to get Nelson to spare ships for it was a marvel,' he added quickly. 'How was it managed?'

The corners of Ball's mouth twitched. 'The Admiral was looking unwell towards the end of the banquet,' he said gravely. 'Only Troubridge and I noticed it, and we got him out of there *magno cum impeto*, drowning his feeble protests with our clamour of concern. Most of the guests were too drunk to observe it. A small private room – Troubridge on guard outside to ward off anxious inquirers – myself and the Admiral inside conning your report. I think Nel, poor fellow, was glad to be away from that rabble for a while. At any rate, he accepted my plea of urgency, read your report twice with some return of his old briskness, and said he'd send my orders on board this morning as indeed he did.'

'Bravo!'

'I believe your encomium is deserved. We got him back in his gilded chair next to Lady H. in time for the adulatory speeches. Now, Captain Peard.' Ball's expression hardened. 'You've some repairs in hand, I see. How soon can *Success* be ready for sea?'

'She can sail tomorrow, sir,' Peard replied as formally.

'I shall require you to sail the day after tomorrow, for Malta. You'll have my orders in writing. Briefly, you are to proceed off Salina Bay, land there if the situation still permits, and prepare the Maltese leaders for my arrival, which will be a day or two after yours. I shall want to confer with them without delay.'

'Aye aye, sir.'

'As to Bonici, you'll please to send him to *Alexander* this afternoon, exchanging him for my own steward, Halliday.' Ball stood up, Peard rising with him. 'What force of marines do you carry?'

'Twenty-two and a lieutenant, sir.'

'Between us we'll muster nearly five hundred,' the Commodore said reflectively; he turned at the cabin door and dour formality gave place to an impish grin. 'At least we've troops enough to save your temple of Venus from the French.'

2

An October rain-squall drifted away eastward as *Success* closed the coast. The morning sun flashed out from behind a cloud to set her wet decks gleaming and conjure intermittent rainbows from the spray that broke under her beakhead. It lit the sliver of white on the southern horizon that was (according to the complacent Macauley) the north-west coast of Malta between Amrax Point and Salina Bay; and the frigate's captain, watching the low cliffs grow beyond the dark-blue chop of the waves, was conscious of an illogical feeling of homecoming. This cool breezy morning was very different from the windless heat of six weeks ago.

Much could have happened in six weeks. The French might have issued in strength from the Valletta fortifications to sweep the island clear of resistance, *Daphne* and *Justice* might be at sea to intercept any British approach. Peard had his keenest lookouts at fore and main and Fossett was on his toes to clear away for action. But as *Success* closed the coast not a sail showed to south-eastward where Valletta lay. Slowly the shore-line ahead rose from the sea, until the twin towers above Salina Bay could be made out from the deck. A hail came from the masthead.

'Cap'n, sir! A deal o' folk on the cliffs right ahead, sir.' A pause. 'They don't look like sojers, though.'

Peard took his telescope to the masthead to see for himself. The tiny figures discernible on the Salina cliffs, grouped or moving, were certainly no ordered body of troops. As he watched, the frigate fast drawing nearer, other figures joined them until there were a hundred or more on the cliff-tops;

many of them, as he was soon able to see, were waving their arms. Below within the bay there was movement, too, half-a-dozen small craft hoisting sail and putting out to meet him. By the time *Success* had come within a mile of the coast these fishing-boats, each laden with as many yelling Maltese as she could carry, were tacking across her course a musket-shot away.

Peard slid down to the deck, where Fossett was screeching wrathfully through his speaking-trumpet.

'Keep clear there, damn your eyes! Keep – ' Here he realized that he was not understood and changed his language. 'Keepee clear or I makee bang-bang and you're bloody well sunk!'

'Very well, Mr Fossett,' said Peard. 'Strip to tops'ls, if you please. Mr Macaulay, I shall anchor in ten fathoms between the capes, as we did last time.'

Success slid on under her reduced sail with the familiar serrations of the low cliffs rising sunlit ahead, and the Maltese craft, wheeling like a flight of pigeons, escorted her on either hand. The yelling of their occupants – it was unmistakably a joyful and welcoming yell – had changed to a rhythmic chanting, two or three words repeated over and over again. The unmeaning sound reminded Peard that he had no Boney to rely on as interpreter now and would have to make his wishes known as best he could. He had concise instructions from Ball and his aim was to find Emmanuele Vitale and pass them on as soon as possible. If he could locate Boney's uncle, no doubt Kazan would guide or take him to Tal-Marfa.

Macaulay, with the hand-compass against his nose, raised a hand; Peard barked an order, the shouts of Fossett and Wrench woke echoes from the headlands on either hand, and the splash of the anchor was followed by the roar of the cable in the hawsepipe. *Success* lay to her anchor midway between Ras Il-Challis and Ras Il-Qawra, as she had first done nearly ten weeks ago. From the ruined towers above, where the people on the cliff-top had gathered, came the same unending chant which the men in the fishing-boats were still shouting.

The ferocious gestures of the first lieutenant were keeping the boats from coming alongside as they plainly wished to do, but their helmsmen steered as close as they dared, turning and twisting with consummate skill. Jacques's marines were forming on the afterdeck as ordered when Peard came up from putting on his best coat for the shore trip; this was in effect an embassy and he would take the cutter and the marines.

'Pulling-boat heading for us, sir,' Fossett said as the lieutenant of marines approached.

'Your glass, if you please. Thank you.' Peard handed back the telescope; the figure in the sternsheets of the boat was easily recognisable. 'Cutter's crew stand down, Mr Fossett, and stand by to pipe the side. Please to form double rank, Mr Jacques.'

Emmanuele Vitale, when he came on board to find Peard awaiting him at the end of an avenue of red coats, was unsmiling as ever and looked as if he had not slept for several nights. The pallor of his long aquiline face was accentuated by the black coat he wore, and there were dark rings round the bright grey eyes.

'Welcome aboard, sir,' said Peard conventionally, grasping the cold clawlike hand.

'And you are welcome back to Malta, captain,' Vitale returned. 'As, no doubt, you can hear.'

The noise of chanting had in fact redoubled as he was seen to board the frigate.

'They seem to be repeating one phrase,' remarked Peard as he ushered his guest into the day-cabin. 'May I ask what they're saying?'

Vitale sat down in a proffered chair. 'The English of the words would be "our Malta frigate",' he said indifferently, and added, without a trace of humour, 'I trust their use of the singular case is not prophetic, Captain Peard?'

Peard laughed and turned to get wine and glasses from a locker. 'No, sir. More vessels than one are on their way to help Malta, as you shall hear. First, though – a glass to the defeat of the French.'

'And to our better success henceforward,' muttered Vitale, emptying his glass at a draught.

'You've had but poor success so far, then?'

'Of this you shall be told in a moment, captain. I would prefer you to speak first.'

In addition to his orders and a document which he was to hand over to 'the Chief of the Irregular Forces operating against the French in Malta,' Peard had been verbally briefed by Commodore Ball. While he detailed the British plans Vitale listened in gloomy silence, toying with the stem of his empty glass. The fire seemed to have gone out of him.

'Three ships of the line, a frigate, and a brig,' he said slowly when Peard had ended. 'No troops, no siege-guns. Without those we can do nothing against the Valletta forts.'

'That remains to be seen,' Peard said. 'All the marines from the ships – about five hundred in all – will be placed on shore for land operations while the total blockade at sea is enforced. Commodore Ball may well decide to land some of the great guns for a bombardement of Valletta, but that will be for him to say when he's taken stock of the situation here.'

'And these marines? They will bring their own food?'

'They will, sir – and their billets. It's intended to place an encampment ashore, behind Bugibba bay in the first instance. They'll be well supplied.'

Vitale nodded, frowning. 'That is as well. For I must tell you, captain, that we are already short of food. It is not the least of my anxieties. Supply ships have reached Valletta with food for the French and we have no means of intercepting them.'

'No more supply ships will reach General Vaubois,' Peard assured him. 'He'll be closely blockaded by our three ships while De Niza's Portuguese squadron watches the Sicilian Passage.'

He forbore to mention that the Marquis de Niza had declined to take orders from a British captain whose rank of Commodore was merely a temporary one; which meant that in all probability the Portuguese ships would be off on a prize-taking cruise that would do little to help Malta.

'This Commodore Ball,' said Vitale, waving the bottle away as Peard made to refill his glass. 'He will doubtless remain on board his ship.'

'No, sir. His first lieutenant will command the *Alexander*. Commodore Ball will need accommodation ashore for himself and a small staff.'

'Indeed.' The Viconde's bushy brows drew together. 'I must consider how we shall fulfil his requirements.'

Peard took a deep breath. Alex Ball's conditions, which had the Admiral's backing, had seemed to him inordinate though he could see their force.

'As to those requirements, sir,' he said, 'you'll find them plainly set out in this document.' He passed it across the table. 'Commodore Ball makes it a condition of his landing that he's placed in sole command of all the forces on Malta and given full control of civil and military administration.'

Remembering Vitale's dictatorial manner on his previous visit he had feared an angry refusal. Instead, the Viconde sat up with his eyes sparkling and his bony face displaying the nearest approach to a smile Peard had ever seen on it.

'Captain Peard,' he said with his old briskness, 'this is good news. I concur without reservation. Hear now my sad story.'

It was a tale of human frailty and incompetence. From the outset the Council of Three had lacked the slightest unity, with Vincenzo Borg and the churchman, Caruana, going their own ways with total disregard for Vitale's meticulous planning. On his own initiative Borg had led three rash and indeed hopeless assaults on the walls of St Michael's Bastion which had resulted in two-score Maltese dead and twice as many wounded. The quarrels and intrigues of the divided command had led to lapse of enthusiasm, even refusal to serve, among the farmers and fishermen who made up the island force. The only success, if such it could be called, had been when the French made an abortive sally or reconnaissance and received so hot a fire from hidden marksmen that they had quickly withdrawn into the fortified city.

'We are not soldiers, you understand,' Vitale added. 'Borg has the courage of a bull and a bull's brains. Caruana thinks of nothing but his priests. With Commodore Ball for our general we can be confident of striking an effective blow at Vaubois.'

Peard was not so confident, for all his respect for Alex Ball's capabilities. Ball was a first-rate sea officer, an experienced leader; but whether he could fill the dual post of civil administrator and military general was an open question. Vitale's reception of that doubtful condition, however, had solved the main problem and he proceeded at once to final arrangements. As soon as the squadron was sighted a messenger would inform Vitale, who would thereupon summon Borg and Caruana to confer with Ball at Tal-Marfa. Ball, with Taddeo Bonici as his interpreter, would take up residence at Tal-Marfa, where also a small force of marines would be quartered in the stables. Beyond these simple preliminaries there was little more that could be done.

'One other thing, sir,' said Peard, gathering up the papers that bore the notes for his embassy. 'When you go ashore, you'll oblige me by seeking out Hannibal Kazan of Bugibba. I think he should be apprised of the marines' encampment that will shortly spring up near his village.'

'I will do so,' nodded the Viconde. 'About the eleventh, I think you said?'

'If the wind holds fair I'd expect the squadron to be anchored off St Paul's Island by then. But – forgive my remissness, sir,' Peard added quickly as Vitale rose to leave. 'I've not thanked you for the spars you obtained for me. Nor have I asked after your lady wife.'

'As to the spars, captain, I ask no better fortune for Malta than the chance that enabled me to supply them,' returned the Viconde with a grave inclination of his bald head. 'And the Lady Julia – ' with a quick glance – 'she is well, I thank you.'

'I shall hope to pay my respects.'

Peard followed his visitor out onto the after-deck, where Jacques called his marines to attention as they appeared.

'You accord me the ceremonial due to a governor, I perceive,' remarked Vitale with a touch of bitterness. 'After the eleventh, Captain Peard, we shall be saluting Commodore Ball.' His glance fell in the fishing-boats that still circled the anchored frigate. 'Permit me,' he added, and raised his voice in a torrent of Maltese.

The boats swung round with one accord and headed out to sea. Vitale turned with a shrug.

'These men have not yet realized our plight,' he said. 'We need every fish they can catch and dry if we are not to starve this winter.'

'We shall be able to bring food from Naples, sir.'

'I trust so. When the news of your arrival reached me I was engaged with the collection of food and the distribution to the poorer villagers who are in need.' He paused. 'I am happy to have the assistance of my wife in this task.'

They passed between the rigid ranks of scarlet coats and white breeches, the pipes of Dowd and Tully, bosun's mates, squealed in ritual salute, and the Viconde's boat took him away across the rippled water towards the shingle cove at the end of the bay. Peard watched him go with immense relief. Playing John Baptist to Alex Ball's Messiah was an irksome business, he found; a rôle as alien to a frigate captain as – as that of Lady Bountiful to Julia Vitale. It was impossible to picture Julia sorting loaves and fishes and distributing them to the poor.

'Permission to dismiss, sir?' said Jacques, clicking heels behind him.

He turned, himself dismissing with an unspoken order the vision of Julia as he remembered her six weeks ago.

'Please do so, Mr Jacques.'

The interplay of sun and cloud-shadow on the golden cliffs, the blue-green water and the fresh cool air, made him feel at home in this anchorage. Except that there wasn't a seagull to be seen it might have been an inlet on the English coast. There were still groups of watchers on the cliff-tops but the rhythmic chanting – 'our Malta frigate'; Peard liked that – had stopped some time ago. Far away to northward, beyond the blue horizon-bar that stretched between the headlands, armies were marching and countermarching, fleets manoeuvring, in the larger areas of the war with France, while *Success* seemed fated to stay with this insignificant conflict in Malta. He found himself content with the prospect.

Up for'ard the hands were flemishing-down halyards and priddying sheets under the eagle glare of the first lieutenant. A seaman came trotting aft to strike seven bells. Half-an-hour to noon – and there was a deal to be done. Peard bestirred himself.

'Mr Fossett!' The lieutenant hastened aft. 'After dinner I shall want all boats away. We'll start taking soundings in Bugibba bay in preparation for the marines' landing.'

3

'Hands to lighten ship!' commanded Alexander Ball. 'Overboard with you, Shuldham – you too, Bonici.'

He sprang out of the *carrozza* onto the steep track and Peard and the steward followed. With some forty stone less to pull, Hannibal Kazan's skeletal horse was able to haul the creaking carriage up the hill out of Bugibba at a steady three knots. The two officers, Bonici a pace or two behind, trudged after it. On either hand and behind them the rocky hillside sloped sharply down to the shores of the wide bay, its waters grey beneath an overcast afternoon sky that darkened the facets of the limestone boulders. Above the shore stretched the lines of dun-coloured tents with dots of scarlet moving among them.

'The gods be praised for this morning's rain!' said Ball, glancing down at his silver-buckled shoes and white silk stockings. 'It's laid the dust. I've no wish to meet this paragon of yours looking like a crossing-sweeper.'

'You mean Emmanuele Vitale?'

'I mean Vitale's lady. I presume we shall be presented. From your description, young Shuldham, she's a rare beauty, *rara avis in terra.'*

With some uneasiness Peard remembered that he had been enthusiastic when his friend asked him about Julia. Like Ball, he was wearing his best cocked hat, blue coat, and white breeches, though the conference at Tal-Marfa, towards which they were heading, was to take place without his presence; the Commodore had explained that he wished it to be seen from the first that the power of Britain to aid Malta was vested solely in himself. Ball, he reflected, was a true disciple of Nelson, at least in his promptness of action.

Alexander, Colossus, and *Culloden* had anchored off the bay of Bugibba – St Paul's Bay, as Ball called it – at first light that morning, 11th October. By noon all the 500 marines were ashore and busily pitching camp, and the three 74's were on their way eastward to begin their blockade of Valletta. No guns had been landed from the ships as yet. Nor had anything been seen or heard of the Marquis de Niza and his squadron, the Portuguese marquis being presumably too highly-bred to come within signal-distance of a Gloucestershire landowner's son. Peard had sent off his messenger to Vitale, his knowledge of Ball encouraging him to chance naming four o'clock as the time of the Commodore's arrival at Tal-Marfa, and had contrived to make Kazan understand that his *carrozza* would be needed at three. It was satisfactory to note that he had timed it admirably; they had twenty minutes in which to cover the remaining two miles to Tal-Marfa.

The Commodore halted on a corner of the climbing track that commanded a wider view of the bay behind them.

'Major Trumbull has hoisted the Union flag,' he said, pointing to the speck of bright colour fluttering above the encampment. 'You know, Peard, this could be a historic day if that flag continues to fly over Malta.'

'The island under the British crown?'

'Yes. But the Maltese must ask for it themselves.' Ball's gaze shifted to the brig that lay at anchor in the outer bay. 'I don't like this anchorage. *Bonne Citoyenne*'s exposed there with shoals under her lee.'

'She'd lie better just south of the island,' Peard said. 'But there's no depth there for *Success*. The frigate's worse exposed if a Malta northerly blows up – *grigal* they call it, Boney, don't they?' he added over his shoulder.

'*Grigal*, sir, yes,' said the steward; he rolled his eyes appealingly at the Commodore.

'Come on,' said Ball abruptly. 'We're falling astern.' As they started up the hill again he uttered a few words in Maltese and the steward quickened his step to walk twenty yards ahead.

'You've picked up the language?' Peard said, astonished.

'A handy phrase or two so far but I'll master it before long. Bonici's my tutor and a damned good one. Bonici henceforth, Peard – you'll oblige me by dropping the "Boney". On the lower deck in *Alexander* it seems they were calling General Bonaparte by that name and Bonici petitioned me to do away with it.'

'I'll remember.'

'As to *Surprise*,' Ball went on, puffing slightly as the track steepened near the top of the hill, 'I promise you she won't be at anchor long. If all goes well at this conference I'll have orders for you before you leave tonight.'

The *carrozza* had halted to wait for them on the level crest where the track branched down to the inlet of Salina Bay. The first autumn rains had changed the look of the place, sprinkling the rock-strewn ground with green and giving the rugged landscape something the appearance of the Cornish uplands. Peard noted the mauve and bright orange of autumn crocus sprouting under the flat rock where he and Julia Vitale had sat, that hot noon in early September, and wondered uncomfortably how she would receive him now. The *carrozza*, rocking and rattling, bore them across the uneven limestone furrows, in and out of the watercourse (where now a little stream tumbled) and on towards the base of the line of crags where Tal-Marfa stood in its rock-walled grounds.

His earlier visit, by night, had shown Peard little of the big stone house and his impression had been of a dark and almost deserted mansion. It was different now, for Emmanuele Vitale, apprised of Ball's coming, had plainly determined to receive him ceremoniously. As the carriage jolted in between the gateway pillars two swarthy Maltese posted there made shift to present their muskets, and farther on a platoon of marines, who had marched from Bugibba that morning, were drawn up in front of the row of stables and outbuildings that were to be their quarters. The Commodore gravely returned the salute of the lieutenant in charge as they trundled on towards the massive portico of hewn stone where Vitale stood with two other men.

As naval custom required, Ball got down first from the *carrozza* but Peard was hard on his heels to perform the introduction.

'Commodore Ball, commanding His Britannic Majesty's squadron – ' He paused, at a loss for a Maltese equivalent of *mister*, and took a chance. 'The Viconde Emmanuele Vitale, sir.'

He saw the quick glow of pleasure and surprise as Ball, shaking hands, returned Vitale's formal greeting with a few words of Maltese; Alex had made a good beginning. When Vitale in his turn presented the Commodore to the other two members of the Council of Three it was clear that his task here would be less easy. Vincenzo Borg, burly and bearded, returned a sullen nod to Ball's smile and handshake. Canon Caruana, who wore a black soutane and biretta, was a small thin man with dark eyes smouldering in a narrow face; he barely touched the Commodore's proffered hand and said nothing in response to his greeting.

'Your quarters are ready for you, Commodore,' Vitale said, 'but I suggest we proceed at once to business – with your concurrence, that is.'

'That has my fullest concurrence, sir,' Ball said with gravity. 'Assuming always that your wife will forgive my delay in presenting myself.'

Two serving-men were lugging the Commodore's sea-chest out of the *carrozza*. Bonici, carrying his valise, followed the four men into the house and Peard, nodding to Kazan who was to drive him back to the coast, went in after them a little uncertainly. His part in this mission seemed to be over and he had only to await Ball's orders before returning to his ship. The spacious entrance-hall he remembered as dark and empty was light now and a small group of men and women, servants by their dress, stood at the far end by the foot of a winding stair with an ornate wrought-iron balustrade. Vitale was ushering his guests into the small room on the right of the hall where Peard had first encountered him.

'With your leave, sir,' Ball was saying, 'Bonici will stand behind my chair as interpreter. I have complete confidence in his – '

The door closed behind them. Peard turned to find that one of the servants had advanced and was bowing before him; a handsome fellow and his face was familiar – the groom, Mattei, who had been with Julia when she rode to the cliff-top above Salina Bay. Obeying Mattei's respectful gesture he followed the man to a second door on the right and was shown into a large and well-furnished room where the stone floor was hidden beneath a profusion of oriental rugs and a fire of olive-wood burned in the huge fireplace. An elderly woman in a black dress was sitting at a table under the window engaged in lace-making. Seated on a divan near the fire embroidering on a tambour-frame was Julia Vitale, in a gown of russet velvet.

Though this meeting was a long-expected one Peard found himself unprepared for its impact on his emotions. He had been so sure of his future invulnerability to Julia's undoubted attractions that the idea of steeling himself against them had seemed ridiculous. Yet here he was, thrilling like any silly youth to the mere sight and presence of her. It was exasperating – but there was pleasure in it, too, he admitted to himself as he made his bow.

'Captain Peard, please to be welcome here,' she said in her quaint English, laying aside her embroidery to rise and curtsey.

He crossed the room to take her outstretched hand.

'Madame, your humble servant.'

Impossible to say whether the impulse that raised the hand to his lips was his or hers. She withdrew it and spoke in Maltese to the elderly woman, who came to place a chair for him facing the divan.

'Maria does not understand your language or mine,' Julia said in French, sinking down on the divan. 'Will you converse in mine, sir? You know I am happier in it.'

'*Voluntiers, madame.*'

Peard's customary self-possession seemed to have deserted him. He could not for the life of him think of anything further to say. Julia, however, seemed not to notice his embarrassment and continued as though there had been no awkward pause.

'It appears we are to entertain one another until this council of war has ended. Then Emmanuele will bring the men in here, we shall take wine, and I shall meet your Commodore Ball. Tell me, sir – what manner of man is he?'

'You must judge for yourself, madame,' said Peard, pulling himself together. 'I can say only that no man could be better fitted for his present task.'

'He is strong? Firm?'

'As iron, *madame.*'

'He will need to be,' she said, frowning. 'There is dissension here.'

As if to confirm her words, there came from the next room the sound of a deep harsh voice raised in what seemed to be angry protest.

Julia shrugged her shoulders. 'Vicenzo Borg – *imbécile brutal*,' she said. 'That wall is a mere partition. But you must reassure me, sir, as the Commodore's hostess,' she went on, leaning forward to lay a hand on his knee. 'I have only the plainest of fare to offer him, for in Malta we have very little food. Will he be content?'

Peard, very conscious of her touch, remembered the gunroom mess in *Zealous* after a long cruise. 'I've seen him eat fried rats,' he said in English.

She grimaced and sat back with a little laugh. '*Tiens!* We have not come to that – yet. Though indeed they say that the poorer folk in Mosta are eating mule.' Her glance at him was suddenly serious. 'But truly, *mon ami*, it will be very bad for us in Malta when the winter comes.'

'I know it, *madame*, and so does the Commodore. He will ask the Admiral to send food from Naples. Your husband,' he added, 'tells me you are helping him in the preparations for food rationing.'

'Oh, I am the dutiful wife *par excellence* – and indeed we must all help when starvation threatens. Perhaps your English sailors and marines will take Valletta and end our troubles. How I should rejoice if they did!'

'But I thought – ' Peard checked himself and began again. 'With your father in Valletta, *madame* –'

'No.' Julia had picked up the tambour-frame and was frowning at the intricate design. 'M. de Boisredin has left Valletta. One of Emmanuele's spies sent the news – a schooner from Ancona brought supplies for Vaubois last week and he sailed in her.' She looked up quickly. 'You will call me *rénégate* – I turn the coat, as you say. I am for you now, Peard, for the British in Malta.'

'I am very glad of it,' he told her warmly. 'I – I would not like to think we were enemies, Julia.'

The swift glance of the brown eyes was enigmatic and a faint smile was on her lips as she fingered the embroidery frame. In the brief pause the hum of voices beyond the partition wall was just audible.

'You have not spoken of what I wish most to hear,' Julia said. 'Now you shall talk while I work at my pattern. Tell me of your doings since last we met.'

The early dusk of a Mediterranean afternoon in autumn was darkening the shadows in the corners of the big room as Peard, collecting his straying wits, tried to make a coherent tale of recent events. With half his fascinated attention on Julia it was difficult. She had dressed her smooth dark hair in some fashion of coils and ringlets that reminded him of his mother, and the gown of russet velvet, though it clung to her and moulded her breasts, had an air of domestic modesty that hardly accorded with the woman he remembered. This was a new Julia. The rosy glow of the firelight played on the curve of her cheek where dark lashes drooped as she bent over her work, on the deft movement of slim white fingers. He felt himself falling under her spell; enchanted. Yes, she was an enchantress. How else explain his feeble resistance to her charm, to –

'That was the third ship's name? *Enchantress*?'

Julia's question broke in upon his feverish musings and sent him into confusion.

'No – no,' he stammered quickly. 'A foolish mistake – *Enchantress* is a sloop. It was *Alexander*, *Colossus*, and *Culloden* that sailed from Naples on the fourth.'

'And the brig *Bonne Citoyenne*, I think you said,' she added with a glance and a smile.

'Just so.' Peard regained command of himself. 'And *Success* was ordered to sail in advance – '

It was quite dark in the room when he had finished his story, and Julia had laid aside her embroidery.

'But you have told me nothing of Naples,' she said. 'It is an age since I was there. Wait, though – ' She turned to speak to Maria, who rose and went out. 'We must have lights, *mon ami* Peard, though I know too well that firelight is more flattering to an ageing lady.'

'You are beautiful by any light, Julia,' said Peard, leaning forward. 'I would – '

'*Chut!*' She laid her finger against his lips. 'Leave the flattery to the firelight, I beg.'

Mattei came in bearing a stepladder and a taper and proceeded to light the candles in the big chandelier that hung from the ceiling. Julia called after him in Maltese as he went out.

'I tell Mattei to be ready with the wine,' she said to Peard.

'The good God knows how long they will talk in there, but they will be dry afterwards, *bien sûr*. Now tell me about Naples.'

For half-an-hour they talked, of Naples a little, of Peard and his ship a great deal. Maria had not returned; perhaps, Peard thought, she had been told not to come back. But though, irresistibly impelled, he twice attempted to move this *tête-à-tête* into a more intimate and passionate course he was gently but firmly steered back to less dangerous waters. The repulses served only to remove the last scruples that struggled to assert themselves at the back of his mind.

By way of the blockading ships and the marines billeted at Tal-Marfa they had come back to Alexander Ball and his dealings with the Maltese language.

'He has a gift for tongues,' said Peard, momentarily diverted from his infatuation by talking of his friend. 'His French is at least as good as mine. And he is an amateur of archaeology. When I told him I had heard of a ruin presumed to have a temple of Venus – '

He stopped abruptly. Julia smiled.

'You remembered that, it appears,' she said in a low voice.

Peard swung himself from the chair to the divan and caught her hands in his. Words, English words, broke from him in a torrent.

'By God, I was a fool that day! A fool and a brute. Can you forgive me, Julia? Can you – '

It was a change in the brown eyes so close to his that checked him. He turned and saw the Commodore at a stand in the doorway, regarding them.

'Your pardon for obstructing you, sir,' Ball said to someone behind him. 'One of your rugs – an Ottoman if I'm not mistaken – caught my foot.'

Peard was standing beside his chair by the time Vitale entered the room with the Commodore. Behind them came Borg and Caruana followed by Mattei with a tray of bottles and glasses. It took a minute or two, fortunately occupied by

bows and introductions and formal courtesies, for Peard to
recover his self-possession and he swallowed at a draught the
glass of wine Mattei brought him. Ball's high-pitched voice
came to his ears, speaking French.

'A privilege indeed, *madame*, to meet Calypso in her own
island.'

'But you are mistaken, sir,' he heard Julia say, laughing.
'Gozo is supposed to be the isle of Calypso.'

'Ah – according to Herodotus.' Alex, glass in hand, had
seated himself where Peard had been sitting. 'Now Wolf holds
that the island of Ogygia – '

'Captain Peard,' said Emmanuele Vitale at his elbow, 'I am
in your debt. It is through you that Commodore Ball has come
to Malta, and Commodore Ball is a worker of miracles. Look
yonder.'

He nodded towards the two men who were taking wine
together at the other end of the room. Vincenzo Borg's bovine
face was alive and eager as he talked, and there was an
approving smile on the lips of the listening Canon. Vitale
himself was evidently excited.

'Those two have been at each other's throats for a month
past,' he went on. 'I speak figuratively, you understand.
Tonight the Commodore's tact and masterfulness have
brought us into union. He is a born leader, captain.' He
paused. 'Is he, by any chance, of noble blood?'

'Not that I'm aware of,' Peard said. 'I believe his ancestors
were farmers.'

'Oh.' Vitale seemed rather dashed. 'Come with me and I
will introduce you to my colleagues, captain. Borg, I fear,
speaks only Maltese, but Caruana has Latin, of course, as a
second tongue.'

To Peard's relief he was rescued from what looked like
being a social ordeal by the Commodore. With a murmured
excuse to Vitale, Ball led him briskly away to make his adieux
to the Lady Julia (a glance and a bow were all that was
allowed him) and went out with him into the dimly-lit hall.

Two words in Maltese brought Bonici stepping forward from the shadows with a packet, which the Commodore handed to Peard.

'These to Harrington on board *Alexander*, Captain Peard, if you please,' he said crisply. 'Sail at first light, *magno cum impeto*.'

'Aye aye, sir. Any further orders?'

'Return to your present anchorage and have a boat at the Salina inlet on the morning of the fourteenth. I'll send written orders by marine messenger.'

They walked to the door together. From the portico Ball looked out at the *carrozza*, waiting in the darkness with its single dim and smoking lantern.

'Rather you than I in that craft by night, young Shuldham,' he said with a chuckle. 'Your orders, by the bye, will be for a cruise. The Sicilian passage. I can't trust the Portuguese.' He clapped a hand on Peard's shoulder and added, in an undertone with an edge to it, 'From what I've seen you'll be a deal safer at sea than at Tal-Marfa.'

CHAPTER FOUR

Saint Elizabeth of Hungary

1

The Euroclydon, whose prolonged violence had wrecked the vessel conveying the Apostle Paul to Rome, had lost nothing of its malignity in seventeen centuries. From late October of 1798 to early December its fury rose at intervals, the tempests from north or north-east blowing for as long as a week before they subsided into drenching rain followed by a period of clear weather. They drove across the eight-mile width of Malta island, flattening the marines' encampment which Commodore Ball had moved farther east to Gebel San Pietru, where it was in sight from the western bastions of French-occupied Valletta. They forced the blockading 74's to beat far out to sea away from the lee shore they were guarding, though at the same time they made it impossible for any French vessel to get out of the harbours and highly unlikely that any supply vessel would try to get in. They came near to foundering the brig *Bonne Citoyenne* on her way to Naples with a most urgent request for food to be sent to Malta. And they gave the frigate *Success* such a battering in late November that her ageing timbers gaped with the strain and the pumps were manned continuously, watch after watch.

Success had been at the western limit of her patrol of the Sicilian passage when this *grigal* blew up. Five days later under tattered scraps of sail she was clawing eastward away from the dangerous nearness of Cape Bon with one of her boats lost, swept away by the gigantic seas, and her officers and crew exhausted by days and nights of battle with the gale. When, in clearing weather, the coast of Sicily was sighted on the larboard bow Captain Peard decided to put into the nearest port of any size to try and make good his losses and damage.

The long struggle with wind and sea, calling into play all Shuldham Peard's knowledge and experience as a sea-officer, had done something to restore his self-esteem but had not given him back his single-mindedness. He was a man divided against himself. One half of him was able to see quite clearly that his infatuation with Julia Vitale was blind folly and a betrayal of his cherished loyalties; that whether De Niza was guarding the Sicilian passage or not (and in fact *Success* had seen nothing whatever of the Portuguese squadron) Ball's action in packing him off to sea was the only possible one in the circumstances. The other half, under the compulsion of a desire he could not control, ignored all this and resented the Commodore's interference. Now that the stress of the gales was removed he was sliding back into the mood of frustration again.

Twice since these outpost cruises began *Success* had returned to Salina Bay for orders and each time the orders had been the same: to cruise between a point twenty leagues north of Cape Bon and a point thirty leagues east of Syracuse, with the object of bringing the earliest possible news of any French relief force sailing towards Malta. The marine sergeant who brought the orders to Salina brought news as well. Ball had moved fast. The marines had been landed on Gozo island to invest the citadel there, which had surrendered without a shot being fired.

'The Malts,' as Sergeant Fisk called them, were to a man delighted with their new leader and were enthusiastically drilling under the instruction of marine officers. There had been some probing skirmishes at the Valletta bastions but as yet no major assault. Less encouraging had been the sergeant's account of food scarcity among the island population; the people in the scattered *casals* had no meat and very little bread, and the shadow of starvation was widening across Malta. The *Bonne Citoyenne*, it appeared, had not returned from Naples.

None of this was in Peard's mind as the frigate neared the coast of Sicily. He was thinking of his next arrival at Salina, in the early days of December, and resolving that this time he would go ashore to Tal-Marfa and see Julia. He had no order to the contrary, and if Commodore Alexander Ball didn't like it then Commodore Alexander Ball could go hang himself.

The Sicilian hills grew out of the windwhipped sea, swelling brown and barren above the lower slopes where the wide cornlands lay.

'Girgenti, sir,' said Macaulay, pointing to a conspicuous hilltop town a mile or two back from the shore. 'They've been building a mole to the wee harbour o' Girgenti.'

'Very well,' Peard said curtly. 'Bear away for the hill yonder, Mr Fossett.'

A sudden gleam of sunshine sped across the tossing whitecaps and lit the ruins of Greek temples on the hill's shoreward side. Then the foreshore heights rose to hide the temples and *Success* headed in towards a small port where a waterfront of low buildings was flanked by a fort on one side and a battery on the other. She glided in past the new Mola di Girgenti, built of stone taken from the ruined temples, and her anchor splashed down in the sheltered harbour. A host of small craft lay at the quays, among them three larger vessels busily loading grain. As his eye fell on these Peard's thoughts flew at once to Malta – Julia busying herself with the apportionment of the island's fast-failing supplies. The lading of those three polaccas would be more than welcome there. But of course Ball had sent to the Admiral at Naples for stores and they would arrive any day now.

Ferdinand of Naples, King of the Two Sicilies, had so far maintained neutrality in the European war, so Mola di Girgenti was a neutral port. Peard had to satisfy an excitable harbourmaster, who came dashing out in a gaily-painted boat, that his *fregata* had only put in because she needed repairs after the storm. Then he went ashore in the gig with Wrench and a bosun's mate, Fiori, who could speak Italian, while Fossett supervised the paying of opened seams, fishing of sprung spars, and the hundred other tasks set for the hands by the *grigal*.

The Sicilians of Mola di Girgenti were a surly and suspicious lot and showed no inclination to help him until he showed the gold coins he had with him. His chief need was a sizeable boat to replace, for the time, the cutter that had been lost in the gale. After some search he found what he wanted, with Fiori's help beat the owner's price down to something under twice what the boat was worth, and arranged for it to be taken out to the frigate.

The clouds and showers of the retreating *grigal* had given place to clear sunshine, and the men loading grain into the polaccas were stripped to the waist in the noonday warmth. The work was being supervised by a stout and curly-moustachioed man in a green coat, who doffed a shabby hat in response to the '*buon giorno*' of the English captain.

'Ask him whither this cargo's bound,' Peard told Fiori.

The question from the bosun's mate evoked a torrent of words and another hat-doffing.

' 'E says as 'ow it's a special order from 'Is Gracious Majesty in Naples, sir,' said Fiori, whose Italian father had sired him in Wapping. 'Waitin' orders to sail, seemin'ly, 'e dunno where for. Could be Leghorn, 'e thinks – '

Here the Sicilian interrupted by thumping his breast and indicating that he was *il signor capitano* Bomba, following this with a lengthy and verbose explanation which Peard cut short by touching his hat and walking on with Wrench along the quay towards his waiting gig. Fiori ventured a comment as he followed a pace or two in rear.

'By'r leave, sir – 'im in the green jacket 'ad a tale about King Ferdinan', sir. Summat about 'im collectin' a big harmy. All the grain they can muster is goin' north to feed the harmy, 'e says.'

'That might be so, sir,' said Wrench. 'The tartane we spoke

off Syracuse last week had the same story — thirty thousand men, mostly Neapolitans.'

Peard nodded without replying. From what he had seen and heard of Neapolitans he doubted whether there was a man among them who would stand his ground under fire.

'If it's true, sir,' Wrench went on, 'it means that Ferdinand's coming in on our side.'

'And God help anyone who has Ferdinand for his ally, Mr Wrench. I'd give his thirty thousand for a tenth that number of Maltese.'

The gig took them back to the frigate and for the next thirty-six hours Peard was too busy to give a thought to the King of the Two Sicilies and his demands for grain.

With new canvas on fore and main and some patchy sails on the mizen *Success* pursued the rest of her appointed course, while Mr Broster and his men stitched away on the foc'sle head and Mr Neal's party worked at the scraping and painting of the new cutter. Once again the Mediterranean spread a level blue floor to the encircling horizon and the weather seemed set fair for some time to come. The southward leg from the latitude of Syracuse found the same moderate westerly blowing under clear skies, and in the early morning of 6th December, having encountered no other vessel except a merchant brig out of Catania, the frigate anchored once more in the entrance of Salina Bay.

Peard made ready to go ashore in the gig. His determination to go to Tal-Marfa, to see Julia, was unaltered, and he could tell himself with some show of reason that a personal report to his senior officer was desirable after purchasing a new boat without sanction. Before the gig was in the water, however, a pulling-boat was reported approaching from the inner end of the bay, and even without his telescope he could identify the squat figure of his late steward in the sternsheets.

Boney (now Bonici, he must remember) was changed in more ways than one from the rotund little seaman of three months ago. He was dressed nowadays in a neat dark suit befitting the interpreter and assistant of a Commodore; and its coat hung with noticeable looseness on a rotundity considerably diminished. His plump cheeks were plump no longer, and though his old smile flashed out for an instant as he saluted his one-time captain his broad face reverted instantly to the anxious gravity it had worn when he came up the side. Peard took him into the cabin, where the steward handed over the sealed packet he had brought with him.

'Where's *Bonne Citoyenne*, Bonici?' Peard asked, with his hand on the packet. 'I saw nothing of her in St Paul's Bay as we came in.'

The little man rolled his eyes and spread his arms despairingly. 'She has come, sir – two days ago – with nothing, no supplies, no food. She sail yesterday. The Commodore send her back again to Naples. Oh, sir –' his voice rose piteously – 'Malta begins truly to starve. No food is left. The people grumble because the Commodore promised food and it has not come, sir. In Bugibba already they kill and eat the rats, and at Tal-Marfa it is the same – '

'What's that?' Peard looked up sharply from the half-opened packet. 'The Lady – that's to say, the Viconde's people, the Commodore too, eating rats?'

'Not yet rats, sir, but for three weeks now we eat only half meals. The Viconde has said that Tal-Marfa must take no more food than other houses and the Commodore agrees. Soon, sir, it will be rats, unless – '

'Very well,' Peard cut him short. 'I'll see what the Commodore has to say.'

There was a second sealed packet inside the first, enclosed in the folded sheet that contained his orders. He spread the sheet with a frown and read the first few lines of careful script: *You are directed to proceed with the utmost expedition to Naples and there deliver, by your own hand, the enclosed package to Rear-Admiral Sir Horatio Nelson, K.B.* His glance skipped a line or two and came to a lengthier scrawl below.

Captain Peard: for your eye alone. Nelson has refused absolutely to send food. All is required by his aristocratic friends in Naples. The Citoyenne *has taken my second and most urgent request, warning that the people here will starve unless food is brought quickly, but you must go in* Success *– see the Admiral, Saumarez, Troubridge – use the utmost endeavour. We must have food. A.B.*

There was an added line, obviously written in haste. *I would go myself but that my absence would endanger the confidence I have won from the Maltese. A.B.*

When he had finished reading Peard stared unseeing at the paper in his hand for a full minute, frowning. The order was a forlorn hope and doomed to failure, as Ball, knowing Nelson, must realise. If Nelson had 'refused absolutely' he would never rescind his decision. Not Saumarez or Troubridge, let alone a mere post captain, would move him. There was more than a hint of desperation in the post scriptum note, unlike Alex Ball's customary self-confidence. *We must have food.* That was the core of the message, the sole consideration now. On a sudden thought his eyes widened and gleamed. If it was not too late –

'I shall sail at once,' he said briskly to Bonici. 'Tell the Commodore.'

'Aye aye, sir – and I tell all people our Malta frigate goes to bring us food,' said the Maltese, looking happier than when he came on board. 'I wish the good luck, sir.'

Peard nodded and dismissed him. Good luck he would need, without a shadow of a doubt; but delay could lose him the chance he was about to take. The plan of visiting Julia would have to be sacrificed to the need for prompt action. And if he returned as he proposed to return he would have deserved her gratitude and admiration, which would make the sacrifice doubly worth while.

He went on deck. The winter sun had not yet risen above the cliffs of the bay and the ruined tower on Ras Il-Challis was black against a pale green sky flecked with small golden clouds. Bonici's boat, on its way back to the inlet, left a rippled wake across waters sheltered from the westerly wind, which had strengthened in the past hour. A foul wind for his course, and likely to freshen still more if that green sky was a true prophet.

'Mr Fossett!' he called. 'We'll weigh at once, if you please. Tops'ls and jib and stand by to make sail the moment she's clear.'

The capstan clanked round, the cable came up-and-down; *Success* made a few fathoms of sternway, felt the wind in her jib, and swung her bows slowly to starboard. Sails flapped and drew taut on the yards as she sheered past the rocks of the Challis headland a musket-shot clear, and came close-hauled on the larboard tack, the first leg of the long beat back to Girgenti.

2

'To and fro, to and bloody fro,' grumbled Boyce, able seaman, ducking under a gout of spray that came over the weather bulwarks where the watch-on-deck were crouching. 'Where's the good of it? An' the pore old *Success* overdoo for a full bloody refit.'

'Divil a refit she'll get this side the Meddy, Jack,' said Sheehy, huddled beside him. 'And if 'tis the good of it ye're asking, why, 'tis to keep the Frinch from coming at Malta island, sure.'

'An' where's the French anyways?' demanded a big topman farther along the row of squatting figures. 'We ain't seen nothin' these three cruises bar feluccas an' a brace o' tartanes, ferkin' nootrals.'

'Nor we ain't had no run ashore,' added another voice.

' 'Oo wants a run ashore when there ain't no gals nor drink nor vittles?' jeered the topman. 'I tell you, matey, I'd give my run ashore for a bang at the Frogs with old iron-arse 'ere.'

He patted the canvas hood that covered the breech of the 12-pounder beside him. Boyce cleared his throat but was careful not to spit.

'Cap'n did ought to 'ave let us ashore at Girgenti,' he muttered. 'Got a fit o' the crabs, I reckon. Not a smile out of 'im since the Commodore landed.'

'Peardy's hankering after his fancy piece, if you ask me,' said a wizen-faced seaman from the other side of the 12-pounder. 'Tom Billings, marine, he saw her – I told you. Sentry ashore, he was, time we was waiting for them spars. Up she comes on hoss-back to meet him, a spanking wench too.' He licked his lips. 'Bosoms like – '

'Away aloft! Reefs in fore and main t'garns'l!' came the roar from aft, and the watch were up and on the shrouds before Fiori came running up with his starter.

On the quarterdeck Peard gauged the effect of the single reef in his upper sails on the frigate's behaviour and decided she was making perhaps an extra half-knot now that the pressure aloft was slightly reduced. The wind had freshened as he expected and *Success* was slashing close-hauled through the ranks of grey-green waves, white-crested, that raced diagonally across her path. A grand sailing wind – if only it had been from south or north instead of west. With a wind like this on the beam he could have covered the forty leagues to Girgenti in eight or ten hours; as a head wind it was going to extend his voyage to two days. And it raised other problems, too.

Peard knew perfectly well that what he was about to attempt was a very dubious adventure in every sense. To commandeer the grain argosy from Girgenti for Malta was a praiseworthy action in one point of view, that of Julia Vitale in particular and of the Maltese population in general; from another, it was plain piracy. Moreover, in disobeying Ball's direct order he was very likely ruining his naval career. It was a measure of his infatuation that in his present state of mind Julia's approbation weighed more than these things.

He had not entirely thrown caution to the winds, however. Mere bullying of the Girgenti authorities would not serve him, nor would the open threat of his 12-pounders; there was the fort and the battery to answer threat for threat, and an exchange of shots between a British frigate and the port of an allied state would break him with the Admiralty for certain. What he had envisaged was a dark night and *Success* hove-to well off the coast, the boats creeping in, the cables cut and the polaccas brought out; the odds were against his managing so much in silence but there was a chance. Now wind and sea seemed likely to make such a plan impossible, for he would never get the polaccas – unwieldy three-masters with a lanteen rig – out past the Girgenti mole in rough weather. Still, there was time for the weather to change before he reached his objective.

In all this, he realised, he was assuming that the polaccas would still be at Girgenti for his taking. Their landing had been about half-completed when *Success* had entered the port, so they would have been ready to sail some days ago. All depended on whether they had received the orders they were awaiting.

Through that day and night the frigate tacked laboriously westward against a strong and steady gale. Morning found her still south of Licata but with the wind veered to west-nor'-west and rain-squalls blowing over. A long reach on the larboard tack brought the Sicilian coast in view from the deck, the hills dark now under a sky of hurrying grey clouds, and by the middle of the afternoon watch Peard's glass showed him the Girgenti hilltop just visible above the notched horizon of the waves. A few minutes later *Success* went about on the starboard tack and the hilltop sank from sight.

'I want to look into Girgenti, Mr Fossett,' he said. 'When we go about next time keep her straight for the port until we're a mile offshore. Then put about.'

'Aye aye, sir,' said Fossett, eyeing him curiously but careful not to comment; the Peard of these days was less conversable than of old.

The frigate, her head four points off the wind, sped close-hauled across the curling furrows on her westerly course for twenty minutes and then came about to head north. Peard took his telescope and went for'ard to climb the foremast shrouds. Up through the lubber's hole of the foretop, up again to the topgallant crosstrees where Muller, the lookout, knuckled his forehead and made room for him on the narrow platform.

'Sir, dis is coldt here,' said Muller. 'You like wear my jacket, *nein*?'

'No,' snapped Peard. 'Take a spell on deck.'

It was cold, and the thin rain driving horizontally across was like a winter's day at home; Muller's long turn up here must have chilled him to the bone. But Peard was not so much concerned with Muller's comfort as his own. When the man had gone down the ratlines he settled himself in the swaying top and for a moment wondered at the impulse that made him want to be up here for this observation of the grain ships. A childish impulse to keep the result to himself? He was thinking of them, he realised, as a trophy to lay at Julia's feet, and that made the next few minutes immensely important to him. But the half of him that could perceive the silliness of it was quickly thrust into oblivion, as always, by the half that was dominated by his passion.

Already the drab outline of the coastal hills was in sight. Girgenti's 'acropolis' thrust slowly up as *Success* raced in towards the land, and as slowly passed from view behind the rising screen of nearer hills. Peard's glass was focussed on the uneven row of buildings above Mola di Girgenti. The pale line of the mole showed in the circle of the lens, and the dark forest of spars along the quays, and then the tautly quivering leech of the fore topgallant sail edged across and screened the view.

'Helm, there! Bear away a point!'

His shout to the deck brought the frigate's head a trifle to starboard and the leech of the sail no longer hid the port. It was little more than a mile away now and he could look above the breakwaters. The fine rain had blurred the lens and he wiped it hastily to look again. There was no mistake. The masts along the quays were all those of small craft, fishing-vessels. He could even see the empty berths at the quayside. The polaccas had sailed.

He knew an instant of bitter disappointment before he hailed the deck. A reckless decision it had been but he had taken it and it had come to nothing.

'Mr Fossett! You may put her about.'

Fossett's screech, tiny figures far below hurrying to the sheets; his lofty perch swinging erect, hesitating in a mighty cracking of canvas, then lying over as the sails filled on the starboard tack. Peard climbed slowly down the weather shrouds to the deck, and as his foot touched the planking four bells of the forenoon watch was struck. Wrench was stepping down from the quarterdeck.

'Those polaccas have sailed, I suppose, sir,' he observed cheerfully.

Peard turned on him a face like thunder and stalked past into his cabin. He might have known Wrench would guess his purpose, he reflected irritably, sipping the hot coffee Halliday had brought him. No doubt the wardroom had discussed it at breakfast; probably the rumour had reached the messdecks by now. In a 32-gun frigate there was no room for secrecy, even of one's own thoughts.

Well, at least no harm was done (something of his old philosophy came to his aid) because he had not committed himself by word or action. *Success* was on her proper course for Naples and all that remained to him was to carry on, to obey Ball's orders though he was totally convinced that nothing would come of them. But daring action planned and frustrated had left him still in an aggressive mood, and he found himself wishing for some enterprising vessel, French or Spanish, to oppose his humdrum progress to Naples. In this at least Jack Boyce and the big topman were of one mind with their captain.

At noon, twelve leagues west of Sciacca, the wind fell right away to a faint but steady breeze, so that the hands ate their peas and biscuit in a comparatively stable equilibrium at the messdeck tables slung from the deckheads. Macaulay, watching the fast-falling glass, prophesied a backing wind and a blow from southerly, and he was quickly proved correct. A reefed-topsail gale on the quarter sent *Success* bowling along at ten knots even under reduced sail, and by the end of the afternoon watch she had made the landfall of Monte Falcone on the westernmost of the Egadi islands, a 2,000-foot hump glimpsed momentarily through flying spindrift and lowering clouds. The frigate brought the gale on her starboard quarter now, heading nor'-nor'-east for Naples 200 miles away.

On the weather side of the quarterdeck Peard paced the slippery deck, hatless and buttoned-up in his pea-jacket. Macaulay and Fossett walked up and down the lee side together, passing the two midshipmen who stood by the taffrail.

'But it willna last,' the master was saying. 'Southerly weather's no to be trusted hereabout. 'Twill be a puff and a piss, as they say in the Minches.'

This remark induced Midshipman West to mutter an inaudible comment in the ear of Midshipman Hepplewhite, who in struggling to contain his mirth emitted a loud explosive sound. The first lieutenant halted and fixed him with a withering glare.

'Very well, Mr Hepplewhite! Up to the masthead with you – crosstrees, mind, and stay there!'

The unfortunate Hepplewhite jerked out his 'Aye aye, sir' and began the long climb up the thrumming shrouds.

'And here,' continued Macaulay, scowling at the interruption, 'comes the piss, as I tell't ye.'

A drenching storm of rain enveloped the frigate from astern and hurtled on past her into the grey obscurity ahead. On the quarterdeck they turned up their collars and continued their pacing. Each time he turned aft Peard noticed that the yellowish pallor that lightened the darkness of the rain-squall had spread, and ten minutes after it had started the squall ceased with surprising suddenness. He could see its long bank of grey-white cloud rushing on ahead, seeming to sweep the hurrying waves clear of mists. A watery radiance from the sun low in the west set the wet canvas agleam; and as though the sudden increase of light had alerted Mr Hepplewhite on his chilly perch aloft the midshipman's urgent scream came down from the masthead.

'Deck, there! A sail, right ahead – two sail, sir!'

Peard had opened his mouth to demand how they were heading when he saw them from the deck. The fleeing squall as it receded left the white-capped sea clear, and its passing had revealed a three-masted vessel some four miles ahead and another farther away, a dark dot just emerging from the grey-white veil. Both were on the same course, crossing his own diagonally. If there was a third, these could be the polaccas – the thought flashed through his mind as he sprang into the weather shrouds.

The first glimpse of the nearer ship through his telescope disillusioned him. She wore a huge lateen sail on the mizen, with square-rig on main and foremast; a xebec, and so was the other. Both were carrying a great deal of sail for this weather. He steadied his glass and was able to discern a row of gunports, how many it was impossible to say at this distance and this angle. Almost certainly they were Spanish and privateers; the xebec rig was a favourite with the smaller Spanish warships, and though they were a long way from Alicante or Barcelona knowledge of Nelson's crippled fleet and shortage of frigates could have tempted them to cruise this far. The farther xebec was clear now, and beyond her another ship, two more – no, three, all with lateens on mizen and main. The polaccas!

'Hands to make sail! Out tops'l reef, hoist topgallants! Lively, now!'

The hands jumped to it. It was weeks since they'd heard that ring in their captain's voice. Macaulay, glancing to windward with a scowl, pursed his lips and nodded dubiously; she could barely carry that amount of canvas at this moment but already the gale was beginning to moderate.

'Starboard a point,' Peard said to the helmsman. 'Steady as she goes. Mr Fossett, turn up all hands. Spray-covers off the guns. Mr Hepplewhite down on deck. And tell Mr Jacques, with my compliments, that we may expect an action within the hour.'

Success heeled more steeply under the pressure of additional sails and buried her nose in clouds of spray, but she was flying like a gull across the tossing water now, visibly closing the distance to the two xebecs speeding across from her larboard bow. On the other bow and clearly in view though farther away, the three polaccas fled under their pyramids of sail, less than a mile ahead of their pursuers. A dull thud came to Peard's ears against the wind, and another followed it.

'Mr Wrench, do you recall how the grain-ships at Girgenti were armed?'

Wrench considered a moment. 'All three the same, sir – a brace of six-pounders a side.'

That agreed with his own recollection; the polaccas were merchantmen and it was a long chance and an unlucky one that had brought these unlikely predators across their accustomed course to Naples. They would have no stern-chasers so the firing had come from the xebecs, who would have long guns at bow and stern. Fossett had returned to the quarterdeck with Tildesley at his heels. Peard addressed them briefly but with the placid good-humour they had so long missed in him.

'The Spaniards yonder, gentlemen, are in chase of the three grain-ships out of Girgenti. I don't know their force – '

'Broadside of ten guns, sir, by my observation,' put in Wrench; with the old Peard back again he felt he could venture an interruption.

'Thank you, Mr Wrench. Twelve-pounders in all probability, which gives them forty to our thirty-two. I intend to spoil their game. Mr Fossett, I shall want the sheets handled with the utmost expedition. Mr Wrench and Mr Tildesley, both broadsides will load with chain-shot, guns at half elevation.'

Two more gunshots, louder than the first, put a double period to his words and he swung round with his glass to his eye. The privateers had closed to within half-a-mile of the three close-huddled polaccas, and *Success* was now less than two miles behind the rearmost Spaniard. The xebecs must have seen him, of course. They had the heavier armament and probably three times his number of men – privateers were invariably overmanned – so their likeliest course of action was to turn from the chase and attack him both together, try to disable his spars so that they could board with their overwhelming numbers. But that would risk allowing the polaccas to escape. Would they hold on and chance the event?

'Mr Fossett, beat to quarters, if you please.'

The surging thunder of the drum; the buzzing chaos of the deck swiftly resolved into order; Fossett reporting, his eyes a-glitter beneath the bushy brows.

'All guns load,' said Peard.

As the 12-pounders rumbled back and forth at the gun-ports the marines, a moving chain of red and white, were climbing the rigging to the tops. Peard turned his glance from the ordered and waiting deck to scan the ships ahead – there was no need for a telescope now. And, by the Lord, he hadn't given his orders a moment too soon. The leading polacca, evidently desperate to increase her speed, had spread additional sail on masts already overstrained by the still powerful wind. Her foretopmast had snapped and fallen to foul her jibs and she had yawed right across the bows of her next astern, who had collided with such force that she too had lost her foretopmast. With two of their intended victims immobilised, the privateers' reaction was inevitable. They bore up together, as though they were joined by a long cable, and came racing towards him on a slantwise course that took them out on his starboard bow; on the next tack, the larboard tack, they would cross his bows.

Peard watched intently. If they manoeuvred in unison they could take him on either beam with their broadsides in passing, and though his own guns would reply he would be far to leeward of the xebecs after the exchange – they would have gained the weather-gauge.

'Hands to the sheets. Quartermaster! Hard a-larboard. – Steady. Thus.'

The frigate heeled violently, the lee rail very near the

foaming wave she had created in her sudden turn across the wind. But Peard knew his *Success* and she came up on the new course prettily, bringing the enemy on her larboard quarter. He had scarcely hoped the Spaniards would be fools enough to do what he wanted them to do; but – perhaps because they were determined to come at him one on each side – they played into his hand. The rearmost of the two xebecs put her helm down and came about, heading now to intercept him, while the other held on. He could deal with them one at a time.

'Starboard half-a-point, handsomely,' he told the man at the wheel, never taking his eyes from the xebec coming up on the beam. 'Starboard again. Thus.'

With their combined speeds the two vessels were closing each other at something like twenty knots. The xebec came on boldly enough considering she was facing a more powerful enemy. He could see her decks crowded with men. He had the weather-gauge and could attack as he pleased, but she must not guess his intention.

'Starboard again, quartermaster.'

As *Success* was heading now the xebec's course, close-hauled as she was, must take her across the frigate's bows well ahead of her; she could rake her on that course, but Peard was almost sure that her tactics would be broadside, grapple, and board, and for that she would be forced to tack. He was watching for the first shiver of canvas that would indicate that she was going about, and the instant it came he roared his orders.

'Hard a-starboard! Larboard broadside – fire as your guns bear!'

Round again swept the frigate, pointing right across the bows of the oncoming Spaniard, now so near that for a moment it seemed that her bowsprit must ram the frigate's stern. The 12-pounders bellowed deafeningly in rapid succession, drowning the noise of the marines' muskets in the tops; through the whirling smoke Peard saw the flash of the xebec's bow-chaser, the only gun she could bring to bear; and then they were past. He ran to the stern rail. The speed of her attack had already taken *Success* well clear, the xebec holding straight on. For a moment it seemed that the Spaniard had suffered no damage. Then, just as her stern-chaser fired, the shot passing astern, the great curved yard of the lateen came down in a tangle of wildly-flapping canvas and cordage, and a few seconds later he saw her maintopmast bend slowly until it snapped the few strands of rigging left unsevered by that storm of chain-shot and crashed down to drag overside. The xebec hung tossing on the waves, dismasted and helpless.

With the cheers of the gun-crews ringing in his ears, Peard turned his attention to the second xebec, fast coming up close-hauled from eastward and not much more than half-a-mile away. A ball from her bow gun pitched half a cable-length ahead of the frigate; despite the fate of her consort and her own inferiority in force, it appeared, she was going to attack.

'Starboard a point,' he told the helmsman, and *Success*, bringing the wind broad on the bow, headed for the Spaniard.

But the threat of attack had been a mere bravado. Round went the privateer in a whirl of foam and away with the wind on her quarter, speeding to the north-east and making sail as she went. Peard nodded satisfaction. He had beaten off the Spaniards without the slightest damage to his ship or his crew, and that was all that was needed. The way was open to his main objective. Two miles to northward the three polaccas were hove-to while the dismasted vessels cleared their damage, their brown hulls lit by a shaft from the red sun that had appeared under the clouds on the horizon. The wind had dropped to a fresh breeze.

'Very well, Mr Fossett. House the guns and stand down. I'll have her stripped to tops'ls and jib, if you please. And I believe we may splice the mainbrace.'

Far astern the crippled xebec had cut herself clear of the wreckage and with jury canvas on the stumps of main and mizen was already diminishing toward the western horizon. He watched her go as *Success*, making more dignified progress under her reduced sail, headed for the grain ships. The hands would grumble at this relinquishing of a certain prize but he had no wish to be saddled with a fourth vessel in his Malta convoy.

3

'You'll take wine, captain?' Peard held up bottle and glass and waggled them interrogatively. *'Si?'*

'Si, si,' said Captain Bomba, his broad face one large smile. *'E eccelente,'* he added a moment later, sipping noisily. *'Egli è un gran pesso che non he ho bevuto di si piacevole, signor.'*

Peard's scanty Italian was not equal to this. He nodded, unsmiling, and hoped that Fiori, who had been sent for, would arrive before his ignorance became embarrassing.

The two were sitting at the table in Peard's day-cabin, Captain Bomba having come aboard two minutes ago in a flood of exclamatory gratitude amid which the word *salvatore*, frequently repeated, was the only one Peard could understand. The lamp hanging from the cabin deckhead swung gently to the frigate's rocking as she lay hove-to half-a-cable from the nearest polacca, Captain Bomba's *Rosmonda*, which had been one of the two to suffer dismasting. It was already twilight and Peard was impatient to sail; the wind was foul for Malta and he doubted the weatherliness of the polaccas. He had sent Neal and a carpenter's crew across to assist in the rigging of jury-masts on the two ships and the job should be finished by now.

There was a knock on the cabin door and Fiori came in.

'Stand here by my chair,' Peard told him. 'Translate what I say sentence by sentence.'

'Aye aye, sir. By'r leave, sir, Mr Neal's back aboard, jury-masts rigged.'

'Very well. Tell Captain Bomba: the polaccas will sail at once, with the frigate as escort. We shall sail for Malta.'

At Fiori's translation of this Captain Bomba, after an instant's gaping incredulity, exploded as violently as might be expected from one of his name, his moustachios flapping with emotion.

'*Silenzio!*' Peard cut him short, scowling blackly. 'Tell him, Fiori, he is to convey this order to the captains of the other polaccas. All three will sail in close company and if any ship fails to keep to my course I shall fire into her.'

The Sicilian, intimidated as much by Peard's fierce glower as by his words, slumped in his chair muttering angrily.

' 'E says the grain belongs to King Ferdinand an' you'll answer to the King for a-stealin' of it.' Fiori hesitated. 'An' 'e says, beggin' pardon, sir, as you're a dirty pirate.'

Peard nodded and stood up, dismissing the seaman.

'Now, *signor capitano*,' he said harshly, 'back on board *Rosmonda* and make sail. *Fate presto* – understand?'

Bomba shrugged and got sullenly to his feet, accepting the inevitable with less fuss than might have been expected. But he returned no reply to the frigate captain's polite *arrivederci* as he went down the side to his boat, and Peard felt some stirring of discomfort. The rôle of bully was not one he could play with ease, he found. The momentary qualm vanished, however, when he thought of Julia, the praise he had earned from her, perhaps the reward – He closed his mind to that with an effort of will. There were fifty leagues between him and Malta and he had yet to bring his unwilling convoy safely there.

It took the better part of an hour to get the polaccas under way, with Fiori yelling orders into the gathering darkness at his fuming captain's instruction. At last, under plain sail and with stern lanterns lit, the four vessels moved in company south-westward into the night, close-hauled on the fitful southerly breeze that had succeeded the hard blow of the afternoon.

The grain ships were in ragged line ahead, with *Success*, a sheepdog herding the flock, paralleling their course a mile to leeward; and in maintop and foretop the frigate's lookouts kept sharp eyes on those distant lights to report if one of them disappeared or diverged from the course. Peard hardly expected that after his threat the Sicilian captains would try any tricks, but he was taking no risks. In taking these illicit prizes, of inestimable value to the Maltese in their present strait, he had stifled his conscience and hazarded his career, and he was determined that nothing should prevent their arrival off St Paul's Bay.

The luck which had favoured the frigate's enterprise so far did not last. Peard had expected a slow passage with the heavily-laden grain ships, but not as slow as it turned out to be. The wind perversely backed to the south-east during the night, and when *Success* and her charges rounded Isola Favignana into the 100-mile narrows of the Sicilian Passage they had a head-wind, light and variable, to contend with. The polaccas, built deep and broad in the beam for cargo, were as unweatherly as he had anticipated and made poor headway against the fickle puffs which the frigate used more efficiently, so that it took them all next day to reach a point 12 leagues east of Pantellaria island.

Peard suspected that Bomba and his fellow-captains were purposely slowing their progress, hoping that chance would provide a Sicilian craft within signalling distance; indeed, he had come so far southward off his direct course in order to avoid any vessels out of Girgenti or Sciacca. However, no sail was sighted that day or the next, when after a night of laborious tacking they came into clearer weather and a steadier breeze. Peard, assessing times and distances with the aid of the chart, concluded that if there was no shift of wind they would be off St Paul's Bay in the early hours of next morning.

In the ordinary way there was nothing of the showman about Shuldham Peard; the marked tendency of Sir Horatio Nelson to 'show-away' was one of the things that blunted his admiration for the Hero of the Nile. But now (half ashamed of himself) he schemed to make an effective entrance with his grain ships for the greater impressing of Julia Vitale. To creep inshore in the dark of a winter's morning would not do.

Before nightfall of that day, when Malta island was no more than 12 leagues away, *Success* closed the polaccas in turn and

told them to heave-to; the new cutter carried Lieutenant
Wrench and the invaluable Fiori across with his orders to
their captains, and three charts, drawn by himself, showing
precisely where they were to anchor on the 10-fathom line in
St Paul's Bay and the location of the shoal near the entrance.
There they would await his further instructions; no one from
the polaccas was to go ashore until these were given. And
through that night, reaching on against the gentle head-wind,
the frigate set a course so unseamanlike in its waste of wind
that Mr Fossett came near to bursting in stifling his urge to
protest. The result of these manoeuvres was that the four
vessels sighted the Malta coast precisely at sunrise.

Contemptible or not, Peard's scheming had the support of
Fortune that morning. The sun climbed into a clear pale-blue
sky, robbing the wind of its winter chill and gilding the low
cliffs above Salina and the rocky headlands of St Paul's Bay. A
Maltese sentinel on Ras-Il-Qawra, where now Commodore Ball
maintained lookouts, sighted the four vessels before they were
hull-up on the northern horizon and long before they closed
the coast the frigate had been identified. The news that 'the
Malta frigate' was back again with three heavily-laden
merchant ships spread rapidly to the *casals* near the north
coast. From Ghargur and Naxxar, from Mosta and Mellieha,
such men as were not on duty with Ball's militia hurried to the
coastal cliffs to watch the convoy's arrival, and with them
came a crowd of children and some women, the latter wearing
the hooded black *faldetta*. As *Success* stood slowly in under
topsails with the polaccas in line abeam Peard's telescope
showed him the throng waving on the cliff-tops: the warmth of
Malta's welcome did something to counteract the gnawing
apprehension of the penalty he had invoked.

North of the Qawra headland the frigate backed her
foretopsail while the polaccas passed slowly into the bay to
anchor as they had been bidden, while on the foreshore below
Bugibba village a small crowd cheered and waved. *Bonne
Citoyenne*, Peard saw, was back at her anchorage south of St
Paul's Island. He saw too that *Rosmonda*'s boat, in the water

even before the polacca's anchor was down, was pulling ashore with a green coat in the sternsheets. So Captain Bomba had chosen to ignore his order. Well, there was nothing he could do about that, and if Bomba thought to appeal to authority ashore he was doomed to failure; no one in Malta was going to release that grain to Naples or Leghorn.

Success resumed the last sea-mile of her passage, rounding the tip of Il-Qawra to her anchorage in the mouth of Salina Bay. The Maltese assembled on the cliffs greeted her with a chorus of shouts which settled into the chant with which they had hailed her three-and-a-half months ago, and the same repetitive song came from the bright-sailed fishing-boats that circled her as the anchor surged out through the hawsepipe.

Peard knew his desire that Julia should be watching this triumphal entry was puerile but he could not repress it. His attention was only half on the busy deck where his lieutenants superintended the squaring of yards and the flemishing-down of sheets and halyards; the rest of it was on the inlet at the bay's end, where his eye had detected a stir and a glint of colour among the little group of people gathered there.

'Mr Neal's ready with his report, sir,' said Fossett, coming up to the quarterdeck.

'Tell him to wait,' said Peard, his telescope to his eye; then – 'Get that swabbers' party off the foredeck, Mr Fossett! All hands without jackets below – and tell Mr Jacques he's to parade his men aft immediately!'

'Aye aye, sir,' jerked Fossett, blinking, and sprang down the ladder shouting.

A boat was putting off from the inlet, a *dghaisa* with an awning aft. He could not positively identify the three passengers but one of them was a woman in a wine-coloured dress.

There was little enough time, not enough for white-gloved sideboys and Peard's best white breeches; but when the *dghaisa* – a high-prowed craft propelled gondola-fashion by a grinning Maltese – came alongside, the frigate's after-deck was set with its two rigid lines of marines and two hastily-tidied bosun's mates with their pipes. Commodore Ball was the first to step over the rail, his long face pale and immovable as a statue's. He stiffly returned Peard's salute and then turned to assist Julia Vitale on board. The Viconde was close behind her but Peard had eyes only for Julia as she came quickly towards him, her claret-coloured pelisse swirling and both hands outstretched.

'*Bienvenu et bien fait, M. le capitaine*,' was all she said; but the glow in her brown eyes (Peard thought) spoke a deeper message.

He had only time for a brief pressure of her finger-tips before the Viconde was beside him expressing gratitude in precise tones that were nevertheless obviously sincere. The Commodore put a somewhat peremptory end to these civilities.

'If madame will permit,' he said, doffing his cocked hat to Julia, 'I have urgent business with Captain Peard. Viconde, you and the Lady Julia would no doubt like to see something of a British frigate.' He turned to Peard. 'Perhaps one of your officers will act as escort.'

'Of course, sir.' Peard's eye fell on his third lieutenant, who was gazing at the lady with his mouth open. 'Mr Tildesley!' Tildesley jumped and went bright crimson. 'Please to conduct our guests round the ship.'

He would have liked to add, in Tildesley's ear, 'and see that no one uses the heads while you're about it,' but there was no time; the Commodore was already heading for the day-cabin.

'Captain Peard,' said Ball, sitting down at once, 'you have brought in a cargo of grain, for which Malta will be grateful.'

His voice was cold and hard, completely expressionless as was his face. Peard, who had been left standing, set his jaw and prepared for trouble. This was Commodore Ball, his senior officer, disciple of Nelson.

Ball laid a folded paper on the table before him. 'So much I've learned from a certain Captain Bomba, who accosted me on my way here and gave me this paper. Bomba states that you threatened to fire into him unless this cargo was brought to Malta instead of the destination for which it was intended. Is that true?'

'Yes,' Peard said woodenly.

'Very well.' Ball paused for an instant. 'You were ordered to sail to Naples, Captain Peard. You disobeyed that order. You know the consequences of that.'

'Yes.'

'Then let me tell you something you may not know. Due largely to Admiral Nelson's persuasions, the King of the Two Sicilies raised an army to oppose the French. As part of the plan, four thousand troops were to be landed at Leghorn in rear of the French army, and Admiral Nelson's ships were to transport them. Bomba's orders – ' Ball laid a finger on the folded paper – 'were to take his grain ships to Leghorn with all speed, their cargo being of vital importance to the commissariat. One may say, Captain Peard, of vital importance to the campaign.'

His piercing grey eyes stared hard at Peard, who met them steadily enough though his composure hid a mind dismayed and shaken. He had subconsciously counted on Ball's condoning his misdeeds in consideration of the urgently-needed relief he had brought; but what he had done went far beyond the condonement of a senior post captain. He had interfered with – perhaps ruined – the plans of kings and admirals. Their Lordships had ordered Admiral Byng to be shot on his own quarterdeck for failing to do his utmost in the face of the enemy. What would they do to Captain Peard? He knew that Ball was reading his thoughts.

The Commodore lowered that stony gaze of his at last. When he spoke, after a pregnant pause, his change of subject startled Peard.

'Saint Elizabeth of Hungary,' he said in the same expressionless tone, 'was a lady given to charitable deeds. Her husband, a powerful lord and probably a thrifty one, sternly forbade her to give any more bread to the poor, on pain of death. Her goodness would not suffer this and one day she set out on her errand of mercy with a basketful of loaves, covered with a cloth. By ill fortune she encountered her husband, who demanded to know what was in the basket. "Only flowers, my lord," faltered the poor lady. But he snatched away the cloth. And behold – the basket was full of roses.' He stopped and rubbed his chin. 'I believe I told that tale tolerably well,' he said in an altered tone. 'Though now I've done so I find its analogy to your own case a trifle far-fetched.'

He glanced up and met Peard's blank stare, half-angry and half puzzled, and the corners of his mouth twitched.

'You don't ask how I come by my knowledge of the Neapolitan campaign, Peard,' he went on quickly. 'I had it from Latimer of the *Bonne Citoyenne*. She returned from Naples last night, empty-handed. Naples was in chaos. Ferdinand's mighty army scattered like chaff before it even met the enemy, the Leghorn landing abandoned, a French army marching unopposed on the port – and the Admiral working in a frenzy to evacuate Ferdinand and all his court to Palermo before Naples is taken. So you see, Peard, that your quite indefensible actions have secured Malta a valuable cargo that would probably have fallen into the hands of the French.' He paused and frowned thoughtfully. 'Ye-es. *Mutatis mutandis*, you have something in common with Saint Elizabeth, I fancy. You agree?'

Peard collected his shaken wits. 'I regret exceedingly disobeying your order, sir,' he said stiffly.

'I believe it may be overlooked this time.' Ball rose to his feet. 'Shall we join your guests on deck?' In the cabin doorway he stopped and turned. 'It's in my mind that you're making a fool of yourself yonder, young Shuldham,' he said in a low voice. 'Don't, for my sake, make a *bloody* fool of yourself.'

CHAPTER FIVE

New Year's Day

1

There was pork and plum duff on the messdeck tables of *Success* on Christmas Day, for Commodore Ball had seen to it that her stores were replenished from *Culloden* and *Colossus*. Much to Ball's dissatisfaction, the two 74's had been ordered to Palermo to assist in the protection of what he called 'Nelson's worthless royalties', with the result that a brig laden with supplies for the besieged French had eluded the weakened blockade and got into Valletta. On the day following her arrival with the grain ships the frigate had been sent to sea again, this time on a closer patrolling course in support of *Alexander* off Valletta; so that Boyce and Sheehy and their shipmates were once more deprived of their run ashore. For comfort they had the knowledge that their Christmas dinners were a good deal more ample than those of the strictly-rationed Maltese.

In a brief colloquy with Peard before he had gone ashore with the Viconde and his wife Ball had disclosed his growing anxieties concerning Malta. The situation, he said, was settling into deadlock. He had early realised the ineptitude of attempting a full-scale siege of the Valletta fortresses using guns landed from his ships as siege-guns; the 64-pounders of the forts prohibited the construction of batteries near enough to do any damage with naval 32-pounders. His force of 500 marines and some thousand half-trained Maltese had no hope of success in an assault of the walls, lacking sappers or the means of opening a breach. As things were, then, it was a contest of endurance, of fortitude in privation. Sooner or later Vaubois must surrender – sooner if the blockade was effective, later if further supplies got through to the French. Help arriving from outside for besieged or besiegers could alter the balance one way or the other but such help was likely to be long delayed.

'The French,' Ball had said, 'know the value of Malta but lack the ships and men to relieve it. The British – which means Nelson, who's given a free hand by Lord St Vincent at Gibraltar – think Malta negligible and won't stir for it while Naples and Minorca are in danger. And if Pitt tells 'em to stir, Peard, it'll be *festina lente* with Nelson, mark my words.'

And yet, he had added, the spirit of his little army of insurgents was so high that he was impelled to make an attack, if only to prevent its lapsing into the apathy of inaction. Some opportunity, some chance that would render success not wholly impossible, was needed.

'And if that chance comes,' he told Peard, 'I shall use every fighting-man I can lay hands on, not excepting your twenty marines and their lieutenant.'

'As their commanding officer, sir, I feel that I too should be present on this occasion,' Peard had said, and Ball had nodded non-committally.

That conversation came briefly to Peard's mind as he walked up and down his slippery quarterdeck in the grey light of a cloudy afternoon. A moderate south-easter was blowing and *Success*, under easy sail, was on the westward leg of her 50-mile beat ten miles off Malta's north coast. That morning she had made signal contact with *Alexander* on her station just out of range of the Valletta forts, and Midshipman Hepplewhite had been bidden to hoist 'Merry Christmas'; to which Harrington had replied 'And a merrier next year'.

Custom required Peard to accept his officers' invitation to dinner in the wardroom but the meal had not been a success. At such foregatherings the tone was set by the captain, and though Peard had made an effort to conform to tradition and initiate cheerful conversation he knew he had failed dismally. For him on this day of all days thoughts of home were inescapable. Insistent mental images of the old house at Penryn on a snowy winter's evening, yellow lamplight in the windows, Lucy and little Tom sitting by the fire, forced their way in like water through a leaky hull. With nearer and brighter pictures of Julia Vitale he tried (as it were) to plug each leak as it appeared, but always another trickle of memory seeped in. It was small wonder that he could not produce the required sociability.

Fossett and Wrench and Jacques did their respectful best to help their silent commander and even Tildesley overcame his shyness sufficiently to relate his experiences when being examined for lieutenant; but as soon as he could do so without discourtesy Peard rose to go on deck, leaving them to finish the wine in a less oppressive atmosphere.

Out in the chill wind with the wet planking underfoot he found it a little easier to stem the trickle of conscience. He could stare out to windward across the dark and ever-changing furrows and tell himself that Julia was not more than a dozen miles away beyond that clouded horizon. On that last occasion when she had come on board *Success* there had been no opportunity for him to talk to her alone; Ball, he thought resentfully, had seen to that. A few polite nothings, another touch of her hand and glance from her brown eyes when she left to go ashore, and that was all. But the glance – he could not be mistaken – had held more than warmth, more than admiration and gratitude. There had been a promise. It recalled the look she had given him nearly four months ago on the cliff-top above Salina Bay, when –

'On deck, there – deck!' came the lookout's hail. 'Sail, fine o' the larb'd bow, sir!'

'Bear up a point,' Peard said to the helmsman; then in a shout to the masthead, 'How's she heading?'

He would have to wait a while for an answer to that. This could be a Frenchman trying to get into Valletta, approaching from the south-west in an attempt to elude the blockade.

'Headin' straight for us, sir – a brig.'

It was a safe bet that she was the *Bonne Citoyenne*, odds that she was bringing him fresh orders. Wrench had come on deck to relieve Macaulay so that he could have a late share in the wardroom festivities.

'The *Citoyenne*'s coming up, Mr Wrench,' Peard said. 'I'll have the topgallants off her, if you please, and stand by to heave-to.'

The brig came hull-up, grew momently as she sped close-hauled across the intervening sea, and a scrap of colour broke from her yardarm.

' "Have dispatches for captain," ' interpreted Mr Hepplewhite, his squeaky voice somewhat thickened by recent celebrations in the gunroom. 'S-sir,' he added hastily.

Success turned into the wind, her backed foretopsail slamming against the mast, and the *Bonne Citoyenne* came neatly about to lie under her lee a pistol-shot away. On the brig's after-deck Lieutenant Latimer waved his hat and shouted, 'Merry Christmas!' and simultaneously a boat shot away from her side. Five minutes later she was off on the same course, and Peard was going into his cabin with a sealed packet in his hand.

You are to anchor off Salina Bay on the 30th, ran Ball's meticulous script, *in such time as will enable you to land at the inlet an hour before sunset on that day. I require your presence at a conference between myself and Sgr. Emmanuele Vitale. A horse will be provided for your journey to Tal-Marfa and return. Latimer will inform* Alexander *of your temporary withdrawal from blockade duty. A.B.* There was a characteristic addendum: *The compliments of the season to you. I find no apple or hawthorn on Malta,* ergo *no mistletoe and –* per saltum *– no Druids.*

Peard wasted little time in speculation as to the reason for this conference; he was bidden to Tal-Marfa – in four days he would see her again. His impulse was to head for Salina Bay at once, to present himself earlier than the appointed time, but his orders implied that *Success* should remain on her station until the time for his landing was nearer. He ordered the frigate on her prescribed course again and passed the rest of the afternoon watch in the evocation of roseate visions. He would touch Julia's hands, look into her eyes. Perhaps there would be opportunity for more than that. Home, Lucy, loyalty, conscience, fled away on the wind and were lost beyond the dark horizon.

2

Halfway up the steep path that climbed from the Salina inlet Peard halted and looked back. The sky had cleared at noon and *Success*, a mile away across the dark-green water, lay between the headlands with her hull in shadow and her upper spars gilded by the light from the sinking sun. The wind seemed steady from the south-east; she'd be safe enough if it stayed there. He went on up the twisting way between the rocks, conscious that his heart was beating faster than the effort of ascent warranted. In half-an-hour he would see Julia.

On the rocky level at the top of the path Sergeant Fisk of the marines, who was waiting with two bony horses, clicked his heels and saluted.

Peard touched his hat in reply. 'Any news, sergeant?'

'None to speak of, sir, cep' the meat rations is finished,' said Fisk. 'These nags is the only 'osses left on the island. The Malts 'ave ate the rest. I ain't much of a 'orseman, sir,' he added as Peard prepared to mount, 'so if it's to be a gallop – '

'A trot at best.' Peard settled himself in the saddle. 'I've been this way before.'

'Yessir? Then you'll know we can't do more than a walk, comin' back after dark, sir.'

Peard nodded and kicked his horse into motion, Fisk riding a few yards behind. The winding track threaded its way through a landscape greener than he remembered it, and the wayside boulders glowed like rubies with the rich light of approaching sunset. But when they had passed the rocky trough of the *weid*, splashing through the little stream that now flowed in its bottom, the sun had dipped behind a bank of cloud on the western horizon and the Ghargur crags rose dark ahead against the sky. The marine sentry at the Tal-Marfa entrance jumped to attention as they clattered in between the stone pillars, but the stables and outhouses beyond, which had housed a platoon of marines, seemed now to be deserted. Peard noted this without interest, for his eager attention was fixed on the portico of the house where he fancied he had seen the flutter of a skirt.

He sprang down from the saddle, and as Fisk led the horses away Julia ran out to meet him. Peard caught her outstretched hands and kissed them.

'Julia,' he began ardently, 'I've waited so long for this – '

'There is no time,' she checked him quickly in French. 'Afterwards, later, we must talk – ' She stopped abruptly and spoke in English, more loudly. 'You are welcome again to Tal-Marfa, Captain Peard.'

Emmanuele Vitale was standing in the doorway. He frowned as Julia slipped past him into the house but the frown vanished as he grasped Peard's hand.

'You are most punctual, captain. That is good. There is matter of import to discuss and we shall waste no time.' He led the way into the big hall and opened the door on the right. 'Much has passed since you first visited me in this room.'

The small room was little changed. Candles were already lit against the fading of daylight and a small fire glowed on the hearth. At the paper-littered table sat the Commodore and (a little to Peard's surprise) his steward Bonici, their heads together over what looked like a sketch-map. Bonici stood up and Ball half-rose to shake hands.

'Your arrival completes our council of war, Peard,' he said briskly. 'Sit down and lend us your aid. Bonici, wine for Captain Peard – for us all, indeed. Before we proceed,' he went on while the steward fetched bottle and glasses from a sideboard, 'I must tell you, Peard, that we four alone have full knowledge of the plan we are discussing. Borg and Caruana have their part to play and that's the extent of their knowledge. We need, you see, to be secret, as I'm sure the Viconde will agree.'

Vitale bit his lip. 'It is necessary,' he said stiffly. 'There is evidence that information of a previous plan was conveyed to the French.'

'With the result that fifteen militiamen were killed,' Ball said sombrely. 'So our present plan, *in hoc statu*, must be doubly secret. The chance I spoke of, Peard, has turned up and we have good hope of success.' He raised the glass which Bonici had filled. 'I drink to Chance — we have need of it. — And fill your own glass, Taddeo, and sit down,' he added sharply. 'You're one of us in this matter.'

The steward obeyed. The Commodore turned to Peard.

'Pray refresh my memory. May of '97 and the battery above Cape Nao. You landed a party from *Success* and blew up that battery, your lieutenant of marines, Jacques, playing a leading part — laid the powder-train and so forth, I believe.'

Peard nodded. 'Slow-match and three barrels of powder, to be exact. Mr Jacques is an expert in such matters.'

'That's what I wanted to know. Now, despatch is the soul of the business, gentlemen, but I wish Captain Peard to be fully acquainted of this plan.'

Ball's high domed forehead glistened in the candlelight as he leaned across the table, his grey eyes alight with enthusiasm.

'The city of Valletta is a fortress a mile square set on a rock peninsula between two deep inlets. On three sides the walls fall sheer to the water or nearly so. On the fourth side, the landward side, is the main gate, very strongly protected by bastions and ravelins. These walls — well, we've probed 'em with a skirmish or two, eh, Viconde?'

'They may be considered impregnable without proper siege materials,' Vitale said with a touch of reproach.

'Just so. The gate is the only weak point. Its defences are such that even if we had a battering-ram — and there's not a tree on Malta big enough to make one — the assault party would never come near it. But it's the weak point all the same,

Peard, because it can be opened.' He paused. 'It can be opened by an armed raiding-party penetrating within the walls.'

'You've found means of ingress?' Peard asked quickly.

Ball's impish grin showed for a moment. 'You abbreviate my careful narration. Yes – a possible means, and for a few men only. The plan, Bonici.'

The Maltese took a paper from beneath the sketch-map he and the Commodore had been examining and Ball laid it before Peard. It was carefully drawn in ink and showed the irregular oblong of fortifications jutting north-eastward between Grand Harbour on its right hand and the long inlet of Marsamuscett on the left.

'The *Guillaume Tell* and the two frigates are lying alongside under the walls in Grand Harbour – here. Across the Harbour in this creek below the houses of Cospicua are three gunboats of a sort – four-pounders mounted in the bows of pulling-boats manned by Maltese. They have my orders for tomorrow night.'

'You're going to attack tomorrow?'

'I should have said the day after tomorrow – the early hours of New Year's Day. But we go too fast.' Ball laid his long thin forefinger on the plan. 'There is the main gate. You see its defences.'

Peard looked closely at the spidery angles and shadings, no thoughts of Julia in his mind now. The gate, he saw, was inset between two big projecting bastions, each with a battery behind and above it. Walled outworks – ravelins – commanded the approaches and there was a ditch along the foot of the walls.

'With all these manned,' he said, 'an army couldn't come at the gate.'

'No. The bastions, St James and St John, are manned throughout the day, sentries mounted at night. In the batteries – they call 'em St James Cavalier and St John Cavalier – they've sixty-four pounders. Now see here.' The long forefinger moved to the left. 'On the south-west corner of the landward walls is St Michael's bastion, overlooking Marsamuscett. This re-entrant wall between it and St John holds the key we've found. You'll see I've marked it with a cross.' He sat back and picked up his glass. 'This is dry work. Pray, Viconde, continue the tale.'

Vitale bent forward, his beak-nosed face intent and frowning. He looked, thought Peard, more anxious and careworn than when he had come on board *Success* a fortnight ago.

'The mark of Commodore Ball,' he began in his precise tones, 'indicates the site of an ancient sally-port. The sally-port, which had an exit at the base of the wall, was closed with masonry by order of the Grand Master a century ago. This I had myself forgotten. I was reminded of it by my wife.'

'The Lady Julia knew of this?' Peard demanded. He felt a thrill of pleasure; Julia had made this enterprise possible.

'But she knows nothing of our plan,' Ball said quickly, with a glance at Vitale.

'She knows nothing of this plan,' the Viconde echoed impassively. 'Like myself, she was born and brought up in Valletta. The old sally-port had a place in her childhood games. From within the walls, steps lead down to it. The wall at the bottom, where once there was a door both narrow and heavy, is now blocked with stones.'

'But the stonework there, Peard, is only a single thickness,' the Commodore put in. 'You see? A well-placed charge brings it down, the assault party enters *ad unum omnes*, the gate is unbarred for the main storming party.'

'The alarm has been given, however.'

Ball turned to the steward. 'How far from the sally-port to the main gate, Bonici?'

'Two hundred and fifty paces, sir.'

'Ninety seconds for a marine at the double-march. Twenty marines and an officer, Peard. That'll be Jacques and his men from *Success*. I've had men of my Maltese militia posted day and night watching these landward ramparts from cover, and we know that the French have four sentries on the bastions through the hours of darkness. When the charge is exploded the alarm's given – yes. But ten marines to deal with the sentries, ten to throw open the gate, and my storming-party pours in, fifteen hundred of 'em, before the French have time to stand to their arms.' Ball threw himself back in his chair. 'Now, Peard – as far as we've gone. Give me your opinion. I'd value it, because I never knew you give a dishonest one.'

The frigate captain considered for a long moment, slowly rubbing his chin.

'If as I've heard Vaubois has four thousand of trained troops in Valletta,' he said at last, 'the odds are heavily against us even in a surprise attack. There's a chance of success but a desperate one.'

The Commodore nodded as if he had expected this.

'And I shall take that chance because we're in desperate case,' he said gravely. 'If we're not supplied from Gibraltar or Palermo within a month we shall starve. The French in Valletta, however, must be in the same straits, or near them.'

'I've two comments to offer,' Peard went on. 'I think there should be a feint attack at the same time as the main one, to draw opposition from the landward side.'

'Good. This is arranged for as you'll hear in a moment. Your second comment?'

'The approach and entry of your storming-party. As I recall it, the landward ramparts stand high and overlook a clear space on the south-west.'

'Half-a-mile of rough ground,' Ball agreed. 'Well?'

'If fifteen hundred men are to be ready to enter as soon as the gate's unbarred they'll have to cross that space before the sally-port is breached. No sentry could fail to see them even on the darkest night.'

'Good again,' Ball said. 'And here again I fancy we shall satisfy you. You must know, first, that tonight all the marines and militia are moving to a forward line under cover of darkness.'

'To the *casals* of Birkirkara and Qormi, two miles from Valletta,' supplemented the Viconde.

'Just so. Major Colborne commands the marines, Vincente Borg the Maltese. By dawn they'll all be out of sight in houses or churches. – But it's time for you and your map, Bonici – likewise for more wine.'

While the Commodore refilled all four glasses, Bonici rose and placed the sketch-map in front of Peard. It showed the area south-west of Valletta and part of the coast-line; the townships of Qormi and Birkirkara were marked, with several dotted lines curling from near them to the Valletta inlets. The steward pointed to the dotted lines.

'Here are *weids*, sir,' he said. 'A man may walk along in them and not show his head above. The soldiers from Birkirkara come by Weid Is-sewdda, Vincente Borg's men from Qormi by Weid Il-kbir, almost to Valletta walls. Here – ' he indicated a point farther north – 'is Tal'Balal, where five ways meet. This is five miles and a half from Salina Bay, sir. From Tal-Balal a mile south, another *weid* goes down to Marsamuscett. There is a good track – '

'Very well, Bonici,' Ball broke in impatiently. 'I'll summarise, Peard. By these *weids* – they were Bonici's idea – marines and militia can move in cover to within striking distance of the gate. That'll be after dark tomorrow night. They'll be ready and waiting to dash out when Jacques lights his fuse. Your second comment is satisfied?'

'Yes.' Peard scrutinized the map. 'My marines, I take it, are to march to this place Tal-Balal and thence by way of this *weid* – ' he looked more closely – 'il-Msida.'

'Just so. It'll take them in cover to the south corner of the Marsamuscett inlet and they can move along the water's edge to below St Michael's bastion. But there'll be a guide waiting for them at Tal-Balal crossroads.'

'I, sir,' Bonici said modestly.

Ball nodded at him approvingly. 'Bonici volunteered for this,' he said. 'He knows that *weid* and can identify the place at the foot of the wall where the old sally-port used to be.'

'If the night be not too dark,' Vitale put in, 'the place may be known by the small oblong of different stonework.'

'We need a night darker than that, Viconde,' Ball told him seriously. 'The moon's past her first quarter and a clear night could sink us.' He turned to face Peard. 'Concerning your first comment, the feint attack. When Jacques's charge goes up the explosion will be heard in Cospicua. The gunboats will put out straight away, firing at the French ships across the harbour. *Alexander* has orders to close the coast at midnight keeping a sharp lookout, and at the gunboats' action she'll open fire on Fort St Elmo.'

'Excellent,' said Peard; he was heart and soul in this plan now. 'So Lieutenant Jacques's powder-charge is the signal for action on all fronts.'

'Jacques is the *primum mobile*,' the Commodore said with a smile. 'He's a reliable officer, I believe, but you must prepare his orders with the greatest care.' The smile faded. 'If he were not at his station at the appointed time – '

'He will be, sir,' Peard interrupted. 'I shall accompany him myself.'

Ball pinched the tip of his nose, frowning. 'I can't allow that, Peard. Your responsibility is to your ship.'

'I believe my first lieutenant is as capable in command as yours is in your absence, sir. May I ask where you will be when the attack takes place?'

'With Colborne's marines advancing from Birkirkara,' Ball said with a sudden grin. 'I'll remind you that your case and mine are not comparable, Captain Peard. I'm commander-in-chief here and your senior officer. However – *finem respice* is our motto in this business and I'll confess your presence with Jacques would relieve me of some anxiety. Very well, then – you've let yourself in for a seven-mile march.' He bent over the map. 'I wish to attack at about eight bells of the middle watch. You'll be marching in the dark. This track from Salina – '

It did not take long to establish a time-schedule. The rough but broad track running south-east to Tal-Balal crossroads shoud take two hours; for the onward route under Bonici's guidance an hour and a half was not too much, since the last half-mile demanded a slow and stealthy approach. Peard and his marines, therefore, would be landed at the Salina inlet half-an-hour after midnight, pick up their guide at half-past two, and be in position below St Michael's bastion by four o'clock in the morning. Peard had a question or two for Jacques's benefit: how thick was the stonework in the blocked-up sally-port, and what sort of terrain lay below the doorway. The Viconde could say only that there was a single course of blocks, probably two feet thick. As to the second query, Bonici said that there was a steep glacis fifty feet in height immediately below the doorway, but this was composed of broken blocks and boulders; a powder-cask could be propped against the doorway stones, he added.

'And now,' said Ball, sitting back in his chair, 'have we covered every point? Viconde? Peard? Bonici?'

Vitale, who was sitting with his chin on his breast, looked up suddenly. 'I feel myself laggard, as you say,' he said. 'Of all present, I alone have no part in this enterprise.'

'Your part is most important,' the Commodore assured him. 'You maintain our headquarters. With respect, sir, you are not a fighting-man. *Deo favente*, the attack will succeed. But if it fails we must have you here to take control.' He stood up. 'Then our council is concluded, gentlemen, and Captain Peard returns to his ship with all speed to prepare his assault-party.'

The others rose, and Peard turned to the Viconde.

'I should like to pay my respects to the Lady Julia, sir,' he said.

The glance that passed between Vitale and the Commodore did not escape him, swift though it was.

'I regret,' Vitale said stiffly. 'My wife has retired early this evening. She is indisposed.'

'I'm sorry,' Peard made himself say. 'I trust she'll soon be recovered.'

Outwardly impassive, he was trembling inwardly with angry resentment. Until a few moments ago Julia and his burning desire to see her had been forgotten in the enthusiasm roused by Ball's daring scheme, but now the disappointment was like a blow in the face.

'Bonici,' Ball was saying, 'see that Sergeant Fisk brings the horses to the portico. My phrase "with all speed",' he went on as the Maltese left the room, 'did not imply a gallop in the dark over that damnable track, Peard. Ride at a foot-pace, I beg.'

Peard nodded shortly and turned to grasp the hand the Viconde extended to him.

'May fortune attend you tomorrow, captain,' Vitale said. 'It is a matter for pride that our Malta frigate takes the place of honour in this venture.' He paused and frowned. 'Commodore,' he added, 'the dispositions after the troops have entered the citadel have not yet been checked. And Captain Peard has not been told of them.'

Ball, who was moving towards the door with Peard, answered over his shoulder. 'You're right, by Jupiter! And we'll check them now. Captain Peard has no need to know them, however, because he'll retire as soon as his party's in through the sally-port – and that's an order, Peard.'

'Aye aye, sir,' Peard said, scarcely heeding him; he was trying feverishly and vainly to think of some plan that would enable him to see Julia.

'D'you remember, young Shuldham, a trifling jest of mine when you got your present command?' Ball asked in a low voice as they reached the door. 'A quotation – " 'Tis not in mortals to command *Success*." Pray don't forget, on New Year's Day, that you're not immortal. Goodnight, and good luck.'

The door closed behind Peard as he stepped out into the big hall. It was empty and chill, lit only by a single candle at the foot of the staircase. Anger smouldered in him. Ball had treated him like a child who had to be forbidden playthings too dangerous for him, cautioned against hazards, cajoled and dictated to by turns. Had Vitale lied when he said Julia had retired? By God, he'd put that to the proof! Moving softly, he went to the door of the room where he had talked with Julia on the occasion of Ball's first visit here, and opened it. The room was dark except for the flickering light of a fire which showed it to be unoccupied. He closed the door and turned to look at the staircase dimly visible in the candlelight, half-minded to mount it and seek her room; but passion had not quite wrought him to the point of madness and he flung the impulse from him with a muttered oath.

As he strode towards the hall door, disdaining silence now, he could hear the clatter of hooves outside where Fisk was bringing the horses round. He had reached the door and his hand was outstretched to the handle when two hands fastened on his arm and he was drawn into a small room on the right of the hall, dark except for the faint glimmer of the night sky through a curtained window.

'Peard,' said Julia's voice in a whisper, 'I had to – '

'Julia!'

She was in his arms, her body soft and warm under the thin robe she was wearing. He held her to him fiercely, kissing her lips, her eyes, her neck, and for a few wild moments she responded to his passion. Then her fists thrust against him, pushing him away.

'No – no,' she said breathlessly. 'Not now, not here.'

'I've waited, I've longed for this,' he muttered urgently. 'And more, Julia.'

She eluded his groping hands. 'You know well this is not the time or the place, *mon cher*.'

'Where, then? And when?'

' *'Sais pas*. Oh, Peard – ' She paused, then laughed softly. 'It is mid-winter and the nights are cool now, but – you remember that morning above Salina, when you shamed me, Peard?'

'I was a brute, an imbecile, a cursed fool of a – '

'Be quiet.' Her fingers sealed his lips. 'Only for you, Monsieur Shuldham Peard, would I say again what I said then. Mattei shall bring you to the place, the ruined temple. He will be at the top of the inlet path at midnight – '

'Julia!' His arms were round her.

'It will be cold,' she murmured, 'but perhaps, *chéri*, we may find a way of warming each other.'

She pressed herself closer, writhing her body against him. Peard's senses were reeling.

'When?' he demanded thickly.

'Tomorrow night.'

Remembrance came with a shock. 'For me tomorrow is impossible, Julia,' he stammered, cursing the necessity of the words.

She drew away instantly. 'So – it is the same thing once more. Your duty, your ship – '

'No!' he countered, grasping her arms so that she winced. 'It is not that, Julia. I am committed to a – a most urgent military action.'

'Ah!' she said quickly, apprehensively. 'Of course – it is tomorrow night they attack the sally-port. I had forgotten.'

'Vitale – your husband – told you that?'

'*Naturellement*. Was it not I who suggested it? But Peard – you will be in danger.' She was close against him, her fingers gripping the lapels of his coat. '*Ah, ciel* – you may be killed!'

'Not I,' he muttered, his lips against her cheek. 'I shall stay alive – for the night after. The night of the first, Julia. We can meet then?'

'Yes – yes. But I am terribly afraid for you tomorrow.' Her voice faltered in the darkness. 'Oh, Peard, I must pray for you. Maria and I will watch and pray that night. You are a heretic and cannot understand, but our prayers must go out at the moment this attack begins, when danger begins to threaten you. It will be at midnight?'

Her sweet solicitude moved Peard deeply. A different Julia this, altogether softer and more womanly than the self-assured beauty of the Salina cliff-top.

'We attack at four in the morning of the first,' he said, stroking her hair. 'But you need not be anxious about me, *chérie*. I am ordered not to enter the walls with the others. And I swear to you,' he went on fervently, 'that the devil himself shall not prevent me from – '

'Be silent!'

She hissed the words in his ear and he felt her stiffen in his grasp. Vitale's voice sounded in the hall, calling out in Maltese.

'He tells Mattei to bring candles to the other room,' Julia whispered.

Peard heard Ball say something to which the Viconde replied, and the voices diminished along the hall. A door opened and closed. Julia pushed him from her.

'Go – go quickly,' she told him.

'Midnight two days hence, then?'

'Yes – now go.'

He kissed her hands and slipped out into the empty hall, out through the heavy door of the portico. Below the steps Sergeant Fisk was waiting with the horses.

'A dark night, sir,' said Fisk. 'Smells like rain.'

Peard grunted. In his present exalted mood it could snow for all he cared. They mounted and rode away into the darkness.

3

By midnight of December 31st the rain forecast by Sergeant Fisk had ceased, having fallen in intermittent south-easterly showers for most of that day. The first hours of the New Year, 1799, found the double file of *Success*'s twenty marines marching along the rough and winding track in the windy darkness, their sergeant, Ragg, at the head of the little column and Corporal Doherty bringing up the rear. A pace or two ahead of Ragg walked Lieutenant Jacques and Captain Peard.

The westering quarter-moon was hidden behind a drift of low cloud; but the cloud was thin enough to let through a faint diffused light, sufficient to disclose the rutted pallor of the track for a dozen yards ahead. The ruts were deeply worn where they crossed the frequent slabs of rock, evidence of centuries of use by the heavy-wheeled Maltese carts, and at intervals a marine would stumble and curse under his breath, bringing a curt growl from the sergeant. Otherwise they marched in a silence broken only by the rhythmic crunch of the marines' boots and the whisper of the wind among the wayside rocks. Jacques was by habit a silent young man, and he and the captain had discussed and rehearsed during the past day the procedures to be followed on their arrival below St Michael's bastion; they had exchanged no more than half-a-dozen words since the longboat had landed the party at the Salina inlet.

The enemy was more than three miles away yet and to windward at that; there was no necessity for a strict silence, and Peard would have welcomed a conversation with Jacques, a man he liked. He wasn't going to initiate one, though, for fear of revealing the confusion of his thoughts. That confusion appalled him. Trudging along shoulder-to-shoulder with the marine lieutenant, he recalled the Shuldham Peard of six months ago, self-assured, undoubting of his own competence, single-minded, imperturbable; and compared him with the anxious and irritable man marching into the darkness of the new year.

The mask of assurance he could still maintain but beneath it was the knowledge that he was a weakling after all. What else was a man who could fling all his cherished loyalties overboard in pursuit of a woman and still open his mind to the protests of conscience? Who but a blatant fool would allow passion to drive him on a course of such dangerous folly? – Thus demanded his rational part, its feeble whining easily drowned by the clamour of desire when he let himself think of his rendezvous with Julia, less than twenty-four hours away now. Nothing could prevent their meeting. Ball himself had ordered him to stay outside the walls when the attack surged in, and no more. He was free to make himself scarce, to be ready for the coming of Mattei to guide him –

'Halt!' said Jacques sharply, stopping. 'Sergeant!'

'Yessir,' said Ragg. 'Change over to next in rear!'

Peard, recalled to the present, waited while the two powder-casks were shifted from the shoulders of a pair of marines to those of the men behind them. It was the fourth time the change-over had been made since the march began, for the casks were no light weight and it had been decided to relieve the carriers every fifteen minutes. The muskets of the new bearers were taken over by the men they had relieved, Ragg growled, 'March!', and they were on their way again. It had taken no more than two minutes, the halts had been allowed for in their careful estimates of time, and yet Peard chafed at the delay. Though his mind was centred now where it ought to be, on the vital business in hand, the turmoil of his other thoughts still seethed on the circumference; and it was this, he knew, that robbed him of assurance. Doubting himself, he doubted the timing of Ball's plan of attack, the feasibility of reaching the foot of the bastion undetected, the efficacy of Jacques's powder-charges against the stonework of the sally-port.

Jacques had expressed some doubt when the plan was put to him. If a powder-barrel was exploded against the foot of the wall, he pointed out, the main force of the explosion would be thrown outward and wasted. But his tentative suggestion that a block should be chiselled out so that a charge could be placed in the cavity was impracticable, the noise of the work being bound to alert a sentry, and in the end he had decided that two small powder-casks, one below each junction of the new stonework with the old, should open a breach. Mr Neal had coopered the casks to the required size, and these with their lengths of slow-match securely fitted had been covered with tarpaulin against possible rain and placed in canvas slings for carrying. Jacques and his under-officers all carried flint, steel, and tinder-box.

'A light, yonder,' Jacques said abruptly.

The dim track had topped a considerable rise where the chill wind blew freely. Far ahead on the curtain of night a spark of orange light showed itself.

'The Valletta fortress,' Peard said.

They moved on downhill and the light vanished. But it needed little effort now for Peard to dismiss his troubled thoughts and concentrate on the immediate future. Another half-hour, he thought, and they should reach the Tal-Balal crossroad and find Bonici there.

These northern coastal lands west of Valletta seemed, as far as he could make out in the dark, to be less rugged than the terrain about Tal-Marfa. The track crossed minor ridges sloping from the right-hand down to the left, and from one of the ridges he sensed rather than saw the black plain of the sea. They had made a fifth load-changing halt, and a sixth, before a downhill curve of the track brought them to a wide uneven space where other tracks could be discerned going off to left and right. A small dark figure stepped forward as Jacques halted his men.

'Bonici,' it said; and one of Peard's anxieties was proved unnecessary.

'Good,' he said. 'Is all well, Bonici?'

He thought the Maltese hesitated a moment before replying.

'All goes well with the plan, sir. I come here now from Wied is-Sewdda, down there.' He pointed to the right. 'Major Colborne and Commodore Ball wait there now, sir, with their soldiers.'

'Have they been there long?'

'Ten, fifteen minutes, sir.'

'Then we're in good time.'

'In good time, sir,' said Bonici, 'but we shall please march on now. I beside you, sir, by your leave.'

The party resumed its march, Jacques falling back to walk with Sergeant Ragg. The way at first led on along the same broad track they had been following.

'Sir,' said Bonici in a low voice as they went, 'there is trouble at Tal-Marfa. The wife of the Viconde – '

'The Lady Julia?' Peard snapped at him. 'What of her?'

'She rode out, sir, with Mattei, an hour after noon. Often in past days she has done so but now, because there are but the two horses to carry messages, this is forbidden. The Viconde is much worried.'

Peard's first apprehensions were quieted. Julia was not the woman to care about prohibitions. Like enough she had taken it into her head to visit the ruined temple of their rendezvous. He felt a pleasurable thrill at the thought.

'Here's little enough to worry about,' he said.

'But, sir,' said Bonici, 'it was sunset when I came from Tal-Marfa and they had not then returned. – This way now, sir,' he added, stepping to the right onto a much narrower path.

'Form single file!' ordered Jacques behind them.

The little path wound downhill through rough terrain where the drystone walls of little fields loomed close at hand and then gave place to dark banks where scrubby plants brushed their legs and stones clicked underfoot. Peard, picking his way down at Bonici's heels, pondered what the steward had said, wondering whether Julia had conceived the idea of being present at the coming attack – perhaps of being near him at the moment of danger. It would be like her, he thought fondly, but he hoped she had not.

'Take care here, sir,' said Bonici.

The path dived suddenly down a bank of limestone shale into a deep gully where a stream burbled in the bottom. They slid down and reformed their line in a roofless tunnel whose walls, clothed in places with bushes, rose well above their heads.

'Change the loads, sergeant,' Jacques said.

'Weid il-Msida,' said Bonici. 'It would be well, sir, to have no talk after now.'

The order was passed down the line and they moved on, walking sometimes on the border of the stream and sometimes in its inch-deep waters. There was some stumbling, for there was little light from the night sky in the *weid*, but for twenty minutes the going was sufficiently easy and they held a good pace. Then the walls of the *weid* shrank in height and stood wider apart, and from close ahead sounded the plash of small waves on a stony beach. The Maltese stopped, halting his followers.

'Here is the shore of Marsamuscett,' he whispered to Peard. 'Scicluna should be here, but he is not.'

'Who is Scicluna?' Peard demanded.

'A watcher, sir, a lookout posted by the Commodore to keep watch on the walls by the main gate. His place was in hiding among the bushes a small way from here. He was to meet us and report. We are perhaps before our time – '

'We can't wait for him,' Peard cut him short impatiently. 'Lead on.'

'Aye aye, sir. With great care and silence, please.'

The party filed cautiously out of the *weid* keeping to the side of a gently-sloping flat of mud and stones across which the waters of il-Msida trickled to the sea. To the left a level blackness of water dimly perceived; to the right an irregular blackness, eroded rocks above the stony beach of the inlet. Bonici kept close in under the rocks. Peard, turning his head to look above them, saw with a shock of surprise the huge shadowy façade of the ramparts already looming against the lesser darkness of the sky.

'Keep your heads down,' he heard Jacques whisper hoarsely behind him. 'Pass the word on.'

The shelf of beach was narrowing below the little crags of the foreshore. Boots scraped on stones, a musket struck against a rock with a dull clank. But the beat and splash of the waves, the repeated thump and growl as they struck the shingle, would surely make the human sounds imperceptible to the ear of a sentry a hundred feet above them. Bonici led the way round an awkward corner of rock where the shingle ended and the sea lapped a few feet below their sliding boots, and then there was masonry underfoot, broad ledges rising to the right from the water's edge. They climbed the ledges, a matter of twenty feet or so, and were in the bottom of a long depression with a bank of earth and stones on one side and on the other a steep slope ending at the base of a great black wall that rose (as it seemed) to the dark clouds overhead. This was the ditch below St Michael's bastion.

Bonici halted a few paces in from the top of the ledges and laid a hand on Peard's arm.

'All to sit,' he whispered. 'And no noise, not one noise.'

Peard passed the order on to the men on his left, though it seemed to him there was hardly need for it. Every man must be aware how hazardous their position was now. Placed as they were at the foot of what appeared to be a re-entrant corner of the ramparts, a sentry had only to look over the wall to see them; the white crossbelts of the marines would ensure their discovery, dark as it was down here. He could tell himself that a French infantryman posted on those windswept ramparts would stand or walk well back from the walls for his own comfort, that if he looked out at all it would be to scan the dark landscape to south and west whence any night attack in force must come. But the feeling of nakedness, of complete vulnerability, could not be banished.

The bottom of the ditch was littered with rock fragments and he heard Ragg's angry hiss as someone knocked stone against stone with a dull *clunk*. They were unslinging the powder-casks and placing them on the topmost ledge; it had been decided that two men should carry them in their hands rather than risk disentangling the harness on what might be a precarious stance at the top of the glacis. Jacques and Bonici were to go up first, to locate the walled-up doorway and find an emplacement for the casks.

'Start away now, sir?' whispered Jacques, looming suddenly at his side.

'Now,' said Peard.

Bonici touched the lieutenant's arm and began to climb the slope towards the base of the corner, with Jacques close behind him. Faint sounds, a slight scraping and the tiny click of a dislodged stone, marked their progress. Peard, craning his head backwards, stared up at the edge of black ruled across the night sky overhead; not a glimmer of light, nothing to indicate the sentries behind the top of the wall. Now the two men had reached the narrow apex of the glacis and the dark figures could be made out huddled at the foot of the corner. Peard found that he had been holding his breath and slowly released it; all was going to plan. He thought of the waiting troops poised to attack, massed in their cover little more than a musket-shot below the ditch-wall at his back. In a very few minutes now their waiting would be at an end.

Bonici was coming down, moving like a black cat on the steep slope. He reached the ditch and crouched beside Peard, breathing heavily.

'Mr Jacques must make level two places for the casks,' he whispered shakily. 'When he is ready – '

He stopped abruptly and turned. There had been a growled challenge – too loud – and now an excited hoarse whispering among the marines at the top of the ledges. Bonici moved quickly towards the disturbance and Peard stood up, every sense alert. The excited voice had spoken Maltese. The steward was back beside him, clutching his arm, whispering urgently.

'It is Scicluna, sir – the watcher. At sunset he saw a man and a woman ride up to the main gate. They were challenged and admitted. Sir – he is sure they were Mattei and the Lady Julia. They will have – '

Peard ceased to hear him. The blow was a thunderbolt that for an instant stunned his senses, depriving him of the power of the thought. But only for an instant. His mind cleared swiftly and beyond the revelation of Julia's treachery he saw the vital need for action.

'Get your men into cover, Ragg,' he said rapidly. 'Down on the beach – you too, Bonici. I'll go up for Mr Jacques.'

He had set one foot on the glacis when from the walls overhead came the blinding flash and crash of musketry. He reeled and stumbled to a hammer-blow on the side of the head and when he got up there was a warm stream flooding down face and neck.

'Jacques!'

Hard upon his yell came a second volley, the glare lighting the slope of the glacis. He saw Jacques, running down towards him, spring high, whirling in midair, and pitch headfirst on a projecting rock. Simultaneously there was a searing agony in his thigh and he fell, rolling into the ditch. The flashes and reports were almost continuous now. They were firing all along the ramparts. The powder-casks! A bullet striking one meant the signal given, the doomed advance beginning.

The wounded leg wouldn't bear him. He crawled on hands towards the casks. A bullet struck a rock fragment in front of him and half-blinded him with dust. A dead marine – he dragged himself across the body and was within a yard of the casks on their ledge above the sea. Immediately on the flash that showed them to him came the blow on his back and the stabbing pain. He got his hands on a cask, somehow contrived to raise himself on one knee, and hurled it outward with all his strength. The other now. He was too weak to grip it, let alone lift it.

The din of firing had gone very far away and he had a curious feeling that he himself was going with it. With a last effort of will he raised the cask and flung it, falling forward as he did so. He heard the splash as from a great distance, felt himself grasped and pulled downwards into cover. Then there was no more firing, no more pain. Nothing.

CHAPTER SIX
David and Goliath

1

Mr Scudamore, secretary to the Commander-in-Chief
Mediterranean Station, closed the door of the great cabin
gently behind him and directed a complacent nod at his
assistant secretary seated at the office table. Mr Scudamore
always referred to this day-cabin on the flagship's larboard
side as 'the office'. He was a tubby little man attired in black
with a neat scratch-wig, twice the age of Mr Knapp his new
assistant, who wore a snuff-coloured suit and his own fair hair.

'His lordship approves,' said Mr Scudamore. 'Indeed, Mr
Knapp, he thanked me.'

The assistant secretary looked appropriately impressed. He
had occupied his present post for less than a month, having
arrived from England on the last day of 1799, but he was well
aware by now that Admiral Lord Keith rarely had thanks for
anyone. Mr Scudamore placed on the table the folder of
papers he had been carrying under his arm and sat down.

'A messenger has gone post-haste to the naval hospital,' he
continued weightily. 'Our man should be here within the
hour. The dispatch in this matter, you observe, has been – um
– unexceptionable.'

'Admirable,' murmured Knapp. 'And an opportune chance
too, sir.'

That the *Queen Charlotte*, alongside the inner mole of
Gibraltar harbour, should be so handy to the new hospital on

the Europa Flats seemed to him a matter of luck. The secretary scowled.

'Mr Knapp,' he said severely, 'never rely on chance. Pursue, pursue, and again pursue – to the bitter-end, as the seamen say. It's my experience that fortune attends only such as pursue their end to the uttermost. I've said this much before.'

Indeed he had. Mr Scudamore had a fine sonorous voice and loved to hear it, especially when it was addressed to a young man who could benefit from his pronouncements. Mr Knapp, sighing inwardly, resigned himself to listen.

'There wouldn't be a better example of what I've been saying,' his senior went on, 'than the present case. Consider it for a moment. A frigate, one of our very few frigates, comes into port with her captain helpless in his cabin, sick of a fever contracted in the West Indies. He is taken ashore and *Success* is without a commanding officer. What would you do, now, Mr Knapp?'

'Promote the first officer,' suggested Mr Knapp, more because he felt it was expected of him than because he thought it would answer.

Mr Scudamore was pleased. 'So. But you must know, Mr Knapp, that a first lieutenant is rarely if ever promoted in rank except after a successful action and with the strong commendation of his captain. The man in our case, Fossett by name – ' He interrupted himself to wag a monitory finger. 'Observe, Mr Knapp, that a memory for names is a necessary aid in our work. To resume. A temporary command for Mr Fossett could be given but will not do, with this cruise to Palermo and Malta imminent. The Admiral requires a post-captain in command and directs me to find one – he, as you know, having only recently taken over the Mediterranean command from Lord St Vincent.'

The assistant secretary did know it. Gibraltar, he had discovered, was full of the gossip and scandal occasioned by this taking-over. Rear-Admiral Nelson, they were saying, was going to find that he could no longer do what he liked with his squadron; old St Vincent's favourite would have to give up his grand friends and his woman at Palermo. He'd already refused to bring his ships away from there and Lord Keith, who didn't like him, would break him for it.

'What, then,' Mr Scudamore was asking, 'is my first action? Where do I commence my pursuit?'

'The files,' said Knapp with some confidence.

'File Twenty-seven,' the secretary amended reprovingly. 'Captains and post-captains at present in the Port of Gibraltar.' He took a paper from the folder. 'This, then, from File Twenty-seven. Byron, Chamberlayne, Moore, Digby – all employed. Hornby awaiting passage to England – with a note that he sailed in *Melampus* yesterday the 25th.' Again the finger wagged. 'Always, Mr Knapp, keep the files corrected. Make the entry the instant, the very instant, the information is received. So, then, File Twenty-seven doesn't help me. According to File Twenty-seven, there are no post-captains available. But do I give up the pursuit? No, Mr Knapp. What do I do? Where shall I search?'

'File Thirty,' said his assistant, who was ready for this one.

Mr Scudamore was annoyed. 'To be wise after the event, young man,' he said with acerbity, 'is – um – well, never mind. I will venture to say that not many men would have thought to consult the list of patients in the naval hospital. I, however, do so. Pursue, always pursue. Remember that. And I find – ' he slipped another paper from the folder – 'I find midshipmen, lieutenants, a master. And one post-captain, Mr Knapp, with his case-history appended.'

Mr Knapp had a brief vision of a naval officer with a written sheet pinned to his coat-tails. He concealed his amusement without difficulty, for Mr Scudamore had a noticing eye upon him even while he consulted his paper.

'A somewhat unusual case-history,' he went on. 'This officer, it appears, was severely wounded on the island of Malta in January of 1799, one year ago, that is. Wounds in head, leg, and chest, ribs broken, lung grazed – I translate the chirurgeon's jargon. Surgeon of *Alexander*, after two months' treatment, recommends patient be sent to Gibraltar. Doubts recovery. Commodore Ball embarks him in brig *Bonne Citoyenne* for transport hither. Brig *Bonne Citoyenne* taken by *Santa Clara*, twenty-gun xebec, eight leagues south of Ibiza. Patient held prisoner-of-war at Cartagena. Cartagena, Mr Knapp is – '

'A port and naval base on the Murcian coast,' said Mr Knapp with relish. 'The Dons have an arsenal there.'

Mr Scudamore stared at him for a moment, tightened his lips, and resumed his exposition.

'At Cartagena. Exchange arranged November with Colonel Bustamente. Patient entered Gibraltar Naval Hospital November nineteenth. Persistent fever but adequate treatment had been given by Spanish doctors during captivity. Treatment continues.' He laid the paper down and eyed his subordinate quizzically. 'Now, Mr Knapp – there's your man. What would you think of him?'

'I should think him devilish tough,' Knapp said.

'Oh, certainly, certainly. I meant as the officer required by his lordship. Head, leg, chest, lung, doubtful recovery – a year's illness. Another man – I say it with all modesty – might excusably have taken the matter no further. But I pursued it, Knapp, pursued it.'

'To the bitter-end, sir?'

'Exactly,' said Mr Scudamore with a suspicious glance. 'In this case, to the naval hospital. I go in person, observe. Never send a messenger on business that requires judgment, Knapp. I go myself, and what do I find?'

His assistant wanted to suggest the bitter-end but decided against it. The question, he apprehended, was rhetorical.

'I find this Captain Peard – for such is his name – nearing full recovery. Doctor Taplin affirms that he mustn't stir from the hospital for another fortnight, but on hearing the nature of my mission the captain declares himself able and willing to be employed on the instant. And for this willingness, Knapp, there was a reason. For I then discover, from Captain Peard himself, that he was in command of *Success* at the very time he was wounded!'

He paused, beaming triumphantly. Knapp was really impressed this time.

'You didn't tell me that, sir,' he said. 'Quite remarkable.'

'I reserved the – um – *dénouement*,' said Mr Scudamore in high good-humour, 'in order to point the moral for your better remembrance.'

'And yet,' Knapp ventured, 'an element of chance can be espied here.'

'I concede it. But mark me, young man.' The finger wagged imperiously. 'The chance wouldn't have been espied at all if I hadn't pursued the matter to the – to its ultimate end. That is the moral I'd have you bear in mind.'

'I'll do so, sir.'

'Good.' Mr Scudamore pulled a watch from his fob and consulted it. 'God save us! Here's noon upon us and we've yet to copy the lists of stores. Pray get them from the locker, Mr Knapp, and use dispatch.'

They had been occupied with the lists for some ten minutes when a marine put his head into the cabin and announced Captain Peard. The two secretaries rose to their feet as a tall man limped in through the door and halted, leaning on a stick. He was gaunt, almost skeletal, and his epauletted coat and white breeches, much darned and stained in places, hung loose as if they had been tailored for a much stouter man. Across the left side of his face from above the ear to the corner of the mouth ran a livid scar, startling in contrast with the pallid skin tight-drawn across the bones of jaw and cheek, which gave him a singularly grim appearance.

'Captain Peard!' Mr Scudamore expressed pleasure tempered with surprise. 'You're earlier than I'd hoped, sir. However, there's no one with his lordship and I think he'll see you now. Will you sit down?' he added, with an eye on the captain's stick.

'No, I thank you.' The scarred mouth seemed to find difficulty in utterance. 'And one moment, if you please. Do I understand that *Success* is sailing for Malta?'

The secretary frowned. 'A service matter, sir, and not to be bruited abroad. His lordship will – '

'Your service matter is common gossip where I've come from, sir,' interrupted Captain Peard harshly. 'The Admiral sails in a week's time with four of the line, three transports, and a frigate, for Palermo and thence to Malta. That's rumour. I merely asked for confirmation.'

'Oh – um – of course, sir, of course.' Mr Scudamore darted a frightened glance at that forbidding countenance and looked away quickly. 'Since so much is known – yes, Malta is the destination, as no doubt his lordship – I'll apprise his lordship of your arrival, sir.'

He started for the inner door, came back for his folder of papers, and disappeared into the great cabin after knocking respectfully. Captain Peard, with a gruff 'By'r leave', laid an extremely shabby cocked hat on Mr Knapp's table and after a second's reflection placed his stick beside it. He was testing his weight on the wounded leg when the secretary beckoned from the doorway; he had not walked without the stick before and it cost him considerable pain and effort to walk the dozen paces into the Admiral's presence without limping.

The great cabin of the *Queen Charlotte*, a 100-gun ship, was a spacious room, whitepainted and austerely furnished. Under the long overhead curves of the deckhead beams the Admiral sat at a table, his grey angular face side-lit by a ray from the January sun striking in at a low angle through the stern windows. He dismissed the secretary with a curt wave of the hand and directed a stony glare at the man who stood stiffly before him.

'Captain Shuldham Peard,' he said, rolling the *r*.

'Yes, my lord.'

'Aye. I have your story here.' Lord Keith tapped Mr Scudamore's folder. 'You've recovered from your wounds, I trust?'

'Yes, my lord.'

'Aye. And you'll have a note from Doctor Taplin for me, no doubt.'

He held out his hand. After an instant's hesitation Peard

produced the folded paper and handed it over. The Admiral's bushy eyebrows drew us together as he read it.

'I read here,' he said severely, 'that in Taplin's opeenion you should not leave hospital for another fortnight at least. He says you're unable to walk without a stick.'

Peard met the penetrating stare steadily. 'Your lordship has observed that I walked in without a stick. Allow me to assure you – '

'Hoot-toot,' said Lord Keith. 'There's a chair behind ye. Sit on it. Now continue with your assurance, Captain Peard.'

'My lord, it's true I'll not be able to run up to the crosstrees for a few days, but I'm fully capable of command. I'm told *Success* is in port and lacking a captain. Your lordship will be aware that a twelvemonth ago I commanded her, until the bullets of the French in Valletta deprived me of my ship. By a chance, and I trust your lordship will consider it a fortunate chance – '

'Nothing of the sort,' said Lord Keith sharply. 'There's nae such a thing as chance, sir. Providence controls these things, let me tell you. There may weel be a Providence in this present conjunction, and that's the reason I'm listening to you instead of sending you packing, back to Doctor Taplin.'

Peard's scarred face took on a faint tinge of colour. 'I beg you'll consider Providence, my lord. I believe *Success* is bound for Malta, and I've sometimes felt that Providence has linked her – and myself also – with the destiny of Malta.'

This was more than a little disingenuous but it had its effect. The Admiral's small bright eyes glinted beneath the grey bristles.

'Oblige me by explaining that, Captain Peard,' he said, leaning back in his chair.

Peard kept his explanation terse. He mentioned the circumstances of his first landing on Malta from *Success* and how this had led to the frigate's mission to Naples and the establishment of the blockade; the seizure of the grain ships (he glossed this over quickly) which would otherwise have fallen into the hands of the French; and his conviction, shared with Commodore Ball, that Malta should in the future become Britain's chief naval base in the Mediterranean.

'Though I've heard,' he ventured in conclusion, 'that Rear-Admiral Nelson takes a different view, my lord.'

'Rear-Admiral Nelson is a fool,' snapped the Admiral; and shot a piercing glance at the captain. 'You'll repeat that to naebody, Peard – understand?'

'I understand, my lord.'

'As to Malta, you and Ball are in the right of it. You may gather my opeenion from the fact that my transports will land Major-General Pigot and a thousand of his troops on Malta. *Success* will sail with the convoy. You will command *Success*.' Lord Keith sat up straight and nodded briskly. 'That's all, Captain Peard. Oblige me by sending Scudamore in here. You shall have my written order before you leave.'

'Thank you, my lord,' Peard said with feeling, rising from his chair.

'Ye may thank Providence,' said Lord Keith drily; then, as Peard turned with a wince and walked awkwardly to the door, 'And don't tempt Providence, man – use a stick!'

2

Captain Peard used a stick. Also he used a lifeline rigged from stern-rail to taffrail on his quarterdeck walk, though the weather remained fair with only a slight sea for the voyage to Palermo, and unusually warm for February. Perhaps because of his refusal to rest it, his wounded leg took a long time to improve though his other wounds hardly troubled him now. The bullet had grazed the trochanter bone, and the lingering pain did nothing to ease the deeper inward wound to his self-esteem, a wound that came near to being mortal. His mental image of himself, unconsciously with him for a score of years, was shattered. Captain Shuldham Peard, competent, dutiful, invulnerable to circumstance and sure of his own worth, had been proved to be an illusion.

The months of pain and fever that lay behind were like a succession of nightmares. He had been only half-aware of his helpless Odyssey, wholly unaware (for the fever had been at its height) of the capture of the *Bonne Citoyenne*. The chance interest of a humane and competent surgeon in the Cartagena prison had saved his life. And it was there, in reviving clarity of mind, that he had seen the unbelievable crassness of his folly.

Nor Hell a fury like a woman scorn'd; Congreve's line recurred again and again in his thoughts as he lay helpless. Of course Julia had never forgiven him; she had waited her chance, punished him and won what she needed at a single blow. Besotted and blinded by passion, he had told her the hour of attack without so much as noticing his blunder, so that armed with that information she could go over in triumph to the French, as she had always intended. He remembered her words to him on the Salina headland, her mention of Jean Gagneraud. Doubtless she was with Gagneraud in Valletta now.

Passion was long dead, jealousy there could be none; but in the vague musings of convalescence he remembered that Gagneraud had been the cause of his landing on Malta – indeed, of his meeting with Julia – and wondered idly whether his destiny and Gagneraud's were in some way linked. Against Julia Vitale he felt no anger at all. Anger and shame burned in him for his own foolishness, and the conviction had grown upon him that unless he could prove himself still, at the least, a good sea-officer he would never begin to regain his lost self-respect.

The hints of Doctor Taplin at Gibraltar that he would be sent home when he was fit to travel roused only opposition in him. He could not go back to Lucy as he was, a man humiliated and uncertain of himself. And when chance – or, according to Lord Keith, Providence – presented the unlooked-for opportunity he had grasped it eagerly.

Captain Rennie, who had been transferred from the *Speedy* brig to take over command of *Success*, was a devout believer in the cat as the prime aid to discipline in a King's ship and his departure was unregretted. Peard's old officers, Fossett and Wrench and Tildesley, had a warm welcome for him; but there was no answering warmth from their captain. An absent nod, a curt unsmiling word, was all the response their congratulatory speeches got from the gaunt man with the ugly scar across his face. Lieutenant Busby, the jovial young man who had replaced Jacques, let the wardroom know his opinion that Captain Peard was a surly scrub, whereat Tildesley gave him the lie and Mr Fossett was hard put to it to prevent a challenge.

'He's in pain,' said Wrench, peacemaking. 'That's it, Mr Busby, depend upon it. Any man in this ship, quarterdeck to lower deck, will tell you there's no better-mannered sea-officer in the Service than Captain Peard.'

'Nor a better seaman, Mr Busby,' Fossett said; and added, 'Four wounds is enough to make an angel ill-tempered.'

But it was not pain that wrought the change they saw, though Peard's watch-below was often rendered sleepless by pain. He held himself aloof because he knew now that he was not the man they had thought him, and his short temper betokened impatience for a chance of retrieving lost honour. Neither logic nor reason supported his conviction that he would find that chance in violent action in the cause of Malta, but this was the blind impulse that obsessed him during the ten-day voyage to Palermo.

Before leaving Gibraltar Peard had learned the news of the past year. Naples was once more in the hands of the Allies. The campaign against the French in Holland had ended in a British defeat. Admiral Bruix's fourteen ships of the line had united with sixteen Spanish battleships and might at any time enter the Mediterranean; a fact which had caused Lord Keith, who had only fifteen ships in his command, to delay his Malta expedition until now. On Malta island the situation was virtually unchanged, General Vaubois and his army still holding out in their impregnable fortress and Ball with his 1,500 besiegers holding them firmly within the walls while such ships as the Admiral could spare blockaded the port. The most recent rumour was of a French relief expedition in preparation at Toulon, where Admiral Perrée's ships included *Généreux*, 74, one of the two ships that had escaped from Nelson at the Nile; and it was this that made Peard double his lookouts when the convoy's slow progress brought it east of the longitude of Minorca. But those ten days might have been a pleasure-cruise for all the action they produced, and the gentle westerlies, giving a fair wind for the passage, supported that illusion. Captain Peard chafed unsatisfied. It was small comfort that he could now dispense with his lifelines and walk the deck with the aid of his stick alone.

At Palermo, after some days of delay, the reluctant Duke of Brontë, as he now styled himself, was detached from his Neapolitan preoccupations and joined Lord Keith's squadron in *Foudroyant, Culloden* also joining. With the flagship *Queen Charlotte, Northumberland*, and the *Lion* 64, there were five of the line to escort the troop transports on the 350-mile passage to Malta. Out to windward and on the flanks of this considerable flotilla *Success* plied her faster course. The weather had changed. A *tramontana* blew from the north, its colder air mingling with the unseasonable warmth that hung over the Mediterranean and bringing days of rain and grey fog with occasional sudden clearances when the horizon might be glimpsed. It was in one such clearance that the seaman at the frigate's masthead hailed the deck.

'Sa-a-a-il ho! Larb'd quarter, sir!'

'How heading?' roared Peard.

'Easterly, sir.' A moment's pause, then – 'Three sail, mebbe four. Could be more on 'em, sir.'

Peard banged the tip of his stick on the deck. 'God damn this leg! Get aloft, Mr Tildesley. See what you make of it.'

It was two bells of the afternoon watch, a grey afternoon of fitful wind and slight sea. Lord Keith's slow-moving ships had passed the south-west tip of Sicily at midnight, and *Success* was patrolling under plain sail three leagues to north-westward of the squadron. The third lieutenant spent several minutes at the masthead and Peard's impatience had risen to boiling-point when he returned to the quarter-deck.

'By God, Mr Tildesley, you took your time!' he snapped.

'Er – yes, sir. I had to – '

'Well? How many and what are they?'

Tildesley licked his lips and spoke in a hurry. 'One of the line, sir, three frigates, six other vessels ship-rigged. In close company, same course as us. The ship-rigged vessels, sir, could be third-raters or transports – '

'Very well.' Peard raised his voice. 'Hands to make sail! Stuns'ls and outer jib, Mr Fossett. Jump to it, there! Bosun, start that man!'

Ten vessels, one of them a ship of the line. On that course and in these waters they could only be Perrée's expedition for Malta, and the ship must be *Généreux*. The sooner the Admiral knew of this the better.

With all the sail she could carry and the light wind over her quarter *Success* sped in the wake of the squadron, sighting them within the hour. Peard was sure enough of his conclusions to rasp an order at Midshipman Hepplewhite, whose excitement was manifest as he hoisted 'Enemy in sight west-north-west three leagues.' The answering hoist at *Queen Charlotte*'s yardarm as the frigate closed her, bidding him report on board, gave Peard a moment's pause. Order or no order, he was not going to make a spectacle of himself for the flagship's people. It had been bad enough dragging himself on board his own ship at Gibraltar, and he refused to entertain the idea of limping across *Queen Charlotte*'s deck with a stick. He made his painful way to his cabin and wrote a despatch for the Admiral, a brief message and even briefer excuses for his non-appearance. As soon as *Success* was under the flagship's lee with her foretopsail backed Wrench was sent across in the cutter.

Lord Keith's reply was merely an order: 'Remain in touch with the enemy.' Wrench, however, was able to amplify this, having had a word or two with the Admiral's flag-lieutenant, who was an old shipmate of his. The squadron and transports were to hold on their course for Malta, now little more than a hundred miles away, and there deploy to intercept the French, who could be assumed to be unaware of the force ahead of them. The flagship and *Culloden* were to join *Alexander*, taking their station just out of gunshot from the Valletta forts; *Lion* was to cruise off the entrance of the Comino strait between Malta and Gozo to prevent the enemy from slipping round by way of the south coast; Nelson in *Foudroyant*, with *Northumberland*, was ordered to chase to windward with *Généreux* as their chief objective.

Captain Peard considered this arrangement critically and found no fault with it except that no special target had been assigned to *Success*. He could hope, and indeed resolve, that he would somehow bring one of those three frigates to action, but he knew that this must depend on circumstances as they arose. As the only frigate in Lord Keith's command *Success*'s duty was all too plain: to attach herself like a shadow to the French 74 and bring Nelson's ships within striking-distance of her. For a frigate to engage a ship of the line single-handed was unheard of, a thing straitly forbidden by Admiralty instructions and bound up with a maximum penalty of death for a captain who wantonly hazarded his ship in such an action. If the 74 was indeed *Généreux*, Peard reflected, she was the lawful prey of *Foudroyant*, for she was one of the only two French ships that had escaped from the débacle of the Nile and Nelson would want to get his hands on her. The other, *Guillaume Tell*, was still shut up in Valletta harbour with the frigates *Diane* and *Justice*.

That remembrance turned his thoughts towards Malta. And while *Success*, her studding-sails and upper canvas taken in, beat slowly back to windward through the gathering dusk he limped up and down the quarterdeck, the heavy thump of his stick accompanying him, letting the past come back into his mind. The episode of his infatuation with Julia Vitale had long ceased to trouble him emotionally. Her treachery to him, his treachery to himself, agonising themes for week after week of vain condemnation, were things past and done with; to

unfold them again would be as useless as trying to recapture
the details of some impossible nightmare. He thought of the
island and how he had felt at home there, of the anchorage
below the Salina cliffs, of Taddeo Bonici and Hannibal Kazan
and their cheerful brown-faced countrymen. And Alexander
Ball. Fossett had told him that Alex had won the passionate
devotion of the Maltese, who looked to him to bring about
their final triumph. He certainly – and through the agency of
Success – had become firmly involved with the island's destiny.
And now once again (Peard told himself) *Success* was playing a
part, albeit a small one, in the winning of Malta. There was
not much that pleased him nowadays but that thought gave
him pleasure.

In the very last of daylight the frigate's lookout sighted the
French topmasts on the northern horizon, and from their
position it was plain that they had made no alteration of
course. They must be heading for Malta – there could be no
doubt now. Peard ordered sail reduced to main and topsails
and course east-south-east, and through a night of rain and
rising wind *Success* steered slowly on a parallel course to that of
Admiral Perrée's ships. It was well gauged, and in the
morning they were sighted at first light, not quite hull-up on
the larboard beam and hidden intermittently by rolling
patches of fog. For the dark clouds had come so low as almost
to skim the long green swell of the waves, and *Success*, her few
sails scarcely filled by a light wind on the beam, wallowed into
and out of drifting veils of mist.

'Amrax Point six leagues sou'-east, sir, by my reckoning,'
said Macaulay in answer to Peard's curt query.

Peard frowned, leaning on his stick and swaying to *Success*'s
corkscrew roll. The French must have seen the shadow-
ing frigate. If they suspected what lay ahead of them and
acted on that suspicion they might bear away north-east
to round Cape Passero. *Foudroyant* and *Northumberland* should
be hereabouts, but with these damned mists playing hide-and-
seek and thickening every hour they might be one mile distant
or ten for all that he could discover of them.

'Larboard two points,' he barked at Fossett. 'I'll have the royals on her, Mr Fossett, and lively about it.'

With extra canvas and the wind broad on the bow, *Success* ceased her corkscrewing and galloped over the swell, converging on the enemy's course. In the last few minutes the French ships had become invisible, for the mists had coalesced into a fog that limited visibility to a cable-length or less. Peard scowled and fumed, staring now into the greyness ahead and now up at the masthead where the lookout had no better view than his captain. In this fog the French could put about and beat back to Toulon without his seeing anything more of them.

'Deck, there! Sail – stabb'd quarter.'

On the quarter! But of course it could be –

'*Fooderant* she was, sir. Gorn now. This bloody fog – '

'How was she heading?' shouted Peard.

'Westerly, sir.'

So *Success* was heading away from *Foudroyant*'s course. Had the British 74 seen him, or seen the enemy? The problem of whether to go about into the mist and seek *Foudroyant* or to hold on towards the French was solved for him before he had time to make a decision. Out of the opacity ahead came the sound of distant gunfire.

'Hands to make sail!' Peard roared. 'T'garns'ls! Away aloft – look lively, topmen!'

Fog could play the mischief with sound, but so far as he could tell the frigate's bowsprit was pointing straight for the boom of cannon, which might be three miles away or perhaps less. One thing was certain: Nelson would steer for the gunfire. *Northumberland* must have encountered the French. Scattered shots thudded, then the dull crash of a broadside. And surely the mist was lightening ahead?

Like a dancer leaping from the wings onto a lit stage, *Success* sped out into a wide sea-plain clear of mist. The furrowed grey-green water stretched to a long bank of fog on its farther side two miles away, and the thunder of the guns was somewhere beyond the wall of cloud. Only one ship was in sight in that cloud-rimmed arena – a big ship, a 74: *Généreux*.

It was something of a surprise to see her on the larboard quarter, but Peard could deduce the reasons behind her presence so far from the main convoy: *Success* had been seen to south-westward and *Généreux* had fallen astern to protect the convoy's flank and rear. At the moment the frigate sighted her she was hoisting topgallants to make for the sound of action, and he recalled Ball's remark that she had escaped scot-free from the Nile battle because she was the fastest 74 afloat. *Foudroyant*, on the other hand, was (he remembered) a slow sailor. He used eye and mind in rapid calculation, estimating the Frenchman's speed under increased sail, his own speed, and the angle of convergence. The frigate's present course would cross that of the 74 at least half-a-mile ahead of her – unless *Généreux* turned away to enter the fog-bank.

'Mr Fossett,' he began, and was interrupted by the lookout's hail.

'*Fooderant*, sir, labb'd quarter!'

Under full sail and wearing her rear-admiral's flag, *Foudroyant* was emerging from the mist a mile away to westward and astern of *Généreux*. Peard saw her make the necessary small alteration of course to head in chase of the French ship, but he knew that unless Rear-Admiral Perrée chose to stand and fight he would draw easily away, perhaps to vanish in the fog-bank.

'Keep your eyes on *Foudroyant*,' he growled at Midshipman West, who was on signal duty.

West's telescope was already at his eye and trained on the British 74, and less than a minute after his captain's unneeded order he was reporting.

'Flag to *Success*, sir – Number Sixteen.'

'Close action, by God!' exclaimed the first lieutenant. 'Sir – '

'I'm aware of it, Mr Fossett. Pipe to quarters.'

Peard's tone was less brusque than usual. Mr West covertly nudged Mr Hepplewhite, beside him, and rolled his eyes meaningly. For the first time since he had come aboard at

Gibraltar Captain Peard was smiling.

3

As if blanketed by the walls of fog that closed in the flat grey plain of sea, the wind had dropped to the lightest of breezes. *Success*, stripped now to main and topsails, moved slowly across the long swell towards the point of interception with the course of the oncoming 74. The ordered tumult of clearing for action had subsided five minutes ago; the 12-pounders of both broadsides were loaded, the matches smouldering on the rims of the tubs, the gun-crews poised and ready. The gunfire in the fog to northward had ceased. Peard spoke into a silence that was broken only by the low-pitched thrumming of the wind and the broken rhythm of the waves along the frigate's sides.

'Mr Fossett! Check that all guns are at full elevation.'

He gave the order without taking his gaze from the big French ship, now scarcely half-a-mile away on the frigate's larboard beam. In a very few minutes *Success*, crossing her course almost at right-angles, would lie dead ahead of her. She had taken in her upper sails and the bow-wave under the high projecting beakhead was barely discernible. He was watching for the first sign of her altering course. She would have to bear up to give him her broadside; her three dozen great guns could dismast him, cripple him, sink him. But before that he would have got his own broadside away. Right astern of *Généreux* and a good mile away he could see *Foudroyant*'s pyramid of canvas coming up but doomed to lose the race if he failed to stop the Frenchman.

'All guns at full elevation, sir,' Fossett reported at his elbow.

Peard did not turn. 'Very well. Larboard broadside will fire at my word. Tell them.'

'Aye aye, sir. – Stand by, larboard broadside!' yelled Fossett.

Slowly the frigate glided forward to cross the bows of the

two-decker, whose towering masts rose almost on her beam and no more than two cable-lengths away. Peard marked the shiver of the foresail and the beginning of the bowsprit's swing.

'*Fire!*'

Instantly came the prolonged explosion of the sixteen 12-pounders, and *Success* reeled to their recoil. Staring through the swirl of acrid smoke, Peard found the story of David and Goliath fleeting through his mind. He had slung his pebble, and for all he could see it had made no impression on the giant. But the great brown flank with its double row of open gunports revealed itself, turning, turning –

'Lie flat, every man! Lie flat!' he roared from the taffrail.

And on his last word came the deafening thunder of a broadside that made his own seem like mere musketry. *Success* shuddered and winced under him as balls smote her hull and overhead the air shrieked with the passing of shot aimed too high. There were other shrieks from her deck, and on the quarterdeck beside him West was staggering about with a hand clapped to a splinter-wound in his arm.

'Get West below, Mr Hepplewhite,' he rapped, and went to the taffrail.

Torn sails, the mizen yard hanging in its slings, but masts unhit as far as he could see. The huge hull of the 74 was astern of him now, turning onto her original course. She could rake him – but it was her larboard broadside again and they'd not have had time to reload.

'Hands to the sheets – stand by to go about! Hard a-larboard!'

Success swung into and through the wind, the turn taking her on *Généreux*'s quarter, and the second broadside from the French guns crashed ten seconds too late, the shot raising a forest of short-lived fountains far out to starboard.

'Meet her – starboard, hard over. Smartly with the sheets!'

Round came the frigate again, bringing the wind on her quarter.

'Get the royals on her, Mr Fossett!' Peard shouted, and spared a moment to look for *Foudroyant*.

The French 74 had not been well handled, and the check required to bring her guns to bear and afterwards resume her course had enabled *Foudroyant* to shorten her distance considerably. She was carrying all the sail she could, and with his telescope Peard could make out a bustle of hands alow and aloft; they were deluging her sails with water, slackening the stays to give the masts play, trying every dodge to win an extra knot from her. But his own task was not yet finished.

A streamer of grey mist from the fog-bank close on the larboard hand drifted across the deck as he turned to look for'ard. Though *Success*'s manoeuvre had saved her it had left her astern of *Généreux*; but she was steadily coming up on the Frenchman's larboard quarter – so steadily, indeed, that he wondered at it. Then the 74 yawed off course a little and he saw that she had no canvas drawing for'ard of her foremast – spritsail and jibs had all been shot away and she was steering awkwardly. A crowd of hands on her focsle-head were toiling to rig replacements. The knowledge that his 12-pounders had not after all been ineffective raised his spirits higher than they had been for a twelvemonth.

'Three feet in the 'old, sir,' said Broster at the foot of the quarterdeck ladder. 'Two shot 'oles on the waterline, both on 'em plugged as best we can.'

'Very well, Mr Broster. – What's this, Mr Fossett – are you hurt?'

Fossett, coming up the ladder with a wet red stain across the front of his white breeches, showed some surprise at the unwonted concern in Peard's voice.

'Nary a scratch, sir,' he replied cheerfully. 'Fuller was alongside me when a ball took off his hand at the wrist. Mr Neal's got a tourniquet on it. Total of four men wounded, sir, no one killed.'

Peard nodded. 'We shall have to stand fire again before we're done.' He glanced aloft, his scarred face wrinkled in thought. 'I'll have the topgallants on her, if you please, Mr Fossett. And send Mr Shorrocks aft.'

As the first lieutenant departed yelling orders, Peard's eye fell on Lieutenant Busby and Sergeant Ragg standing glumly at the rail of the after-deck. There had seemed little point, for this encounter, in sending the marines into the tops and he had told Busby to keep his men below decks. Now, however, he needed them. *Généreux* had to be stopped and he was going to throw everything he had into the attempt.

'Mr Busby, please to get your men aloft. They are to load their muskets immediately they reach the tops.'

'Aye aye, sir!' said Busby joyfully, his round red face lighting up.

'And Mr Busby – every man will aim at the Frenchman's helm, the quartermasters at the wheel. You understand?'

'Yessir. – Sergeant! Marines to action posts, at the double!'

Mr Shorrocks, the gunner, came trotting aft, his long grey locks flapping as he ran.

'Mr Shorrocks,' said Peard. 'I want you to see that each gun of the larboard broadside is given the fullest possible elevation. Quoins out, use wedges if you can. The men will fire on the upward roll, as their guns bear. I shall give the word.'

'Aye aye, sir.'

The men aloft on the footropes had cast off the gaskets and on deck they were hauling the sheets. *Success* took on a more pronounced heel and noticeably increased her speed. Her bowsprit-tip was almost level with *Généreux*'s stern two cable-lengths to starboard.

'Starboard, quartermaster. Steady.'

The frigate came round, bringing the wind on her quarter, and headed diagonally across the French ship's wake to pass close below the high many-windowed stern. A fusillade from the soldiers massed at the poop rail broke out as she came within musket-shot and a bullet ripped blue cloth from Peard's sleeve between shoulder and elbow, grazing the skin. He hardly noticed the searing pain, biding his time.

'Fire!'

The bow gun crashed out, followed instantly by the next astern. Then the succession of explosions ran aft along the line. Simultaneously the crackle of shots came from the frigate's tops. The smoke blew clear to leeward and Peard, propping himself with his stick, gazed eagerly across the widening space of water. Down in a flurry of canvas came the spanker yard – a wild cheer from his gunners – and *Généreux* swung slowly off her course, to larboard. Either the loss of her stern canvas had unbalanced her steering or the marines' bullets had found their target. In either case the respite was only temporary. He had crossed to leeward of the 74 so as to win the extra elevation that *Success*'s leeward heel had given to his single tier of guns, had limited his target to the Frenchman's after parts so that she couldn't reply, her guns not bearing, and had succeeded tolerably well. And now the penalty had to be paid.

Along the deck the gun-crews were feverishly sponging, reloading, running-up their guns. But *Généreux*'s cliff-like starboard side was opening to view, very quickly because she was swinging back to starboard as the frigate crossed her flank. In a few seconds now her 18-pounders would bear on him.

'Sir!' Fossett had come up to report. 'All guns – '

He got no further. The double tier of gunports across the grey water vomited flame and smoke and the air overhead was loud with the screaming of shot. *Success* lurched and reeled to the hammer-blow of 18-pounder balls, her maintopmast toppled and plunged in a welter of canvas and cordage. Six feet of the taffrail hurtled away in a cloud of splinters and from below it came a tremendous crash as a ball struck the wheel and plunged out through the lee bulwarks. The frigate, a scarecrow ship of tattered sails and severed rigging, flew up into the wind and hung shuddering like a wounded horse.

Glancing down, Peard saw the helmsman sprawled in a crimson pool. The man's head was missing. Beside him

Macaulay lay feebly moving, with blood welling from his thigh. Wheel and binnacle were shattered.

'Man the tiller-ropes, Mr Fossett, if you please.' Peard's voice was cool and clear. 'And send two hands aft to take Macaulay below. We must get under way again as soon as – '

'Sir – sir!' Hepplewhite, very pale, was excitedly jumping up and down at his side. '*Foudroyant* signalling, sir – "Discontinue action".'

'Very well. Just calm yourself, Mr Hepplewhite,' Peard said kindly, 'and acknowledge.'

He turned and saw *Foudroyant* a bare quarter-mile away, coming up fast in *Généreux*'s wake. She was a fine sight with all her cloud of sail drawing, pendant and colours streaming on the wind, gunports open in the black-and-yellow chequer of her big hull. She went foaming past the helpless frigate and from her deck came the sound of cheering. On her quarterdeck a slight figure raised his cocked hat with his left hand and waved it aloft. He seemed to be shouting something but Peard could not distinguish the words; Nelson, he recollected, had no very strong voice. He doffed his own hat in reply and watched *Foudroyant* creep up on the French ship's starboard quarter.

Généreux seemed the wraith of a ship, for the fringes of the mist had enveloped her and grey tendrils curled about her masts. Undoubtedly she was in trouble with her steering – she had yawed away after that broadside – but her flank had come round to starboard and she greeted *Foudroyant* with the fume and thunder of three dozen great guns before the guns of the British 74 could bear. Holes appeared in *Foudroyant*'s main and mizen sails, the falling shot raised fountains close to the frigate.

Then came the rolling crash of the reply. The vast dun clouds of smoke mingled with the advancing fog and hid the hulls of the combatants, and he couldn't tell whose was the mast that leaned and fell into the smoke, but he saw the dark shape of a third ship loom out of the mist to the left of the others and the stabbing orange flames of *Northumberland*'s broadside. A single gun spoke after it, and then there was silence; a silence broken by Wrench's bull-bellow from for'ard: 'She's struck! Three cheers, lads!'

The cheers came from the deck where the gunners still stood by their guns, from high on the mainmast where they were clearing and lowering the wreckage of the topmast, and – in a hollow-sounding echo – from under the after-deck where half-a-dozen hands were manning the steering-tackles. Hearing them, Peard smiled; and wondered at himself. Yesterday he would have hauled Mr Wrench over the coals for ordering cheers without his consent. Now – well, what he set out to do had been accomplished and he doubted whether it could have been done better. There were no other doubts – now.

"S-sir!"

It was Hepplewhite again. He hadn't joined in the cheers and he looked terrified.

'I was s-sick, sir,' he piped shakily. 'Over there, sir, by the rail. I c-couldn't help it, sir.'

'Never mind, Mr Hepplewhite. There's some Frenchmen we know of who'll be a deal more sick than you. – Yes, Mr Tildesley?'

'Mr Fossett's compliments, sir,' said Tildesley, 'and can he start the pumps – the water's gaining in the after-hold.'

'Pray tell him he may do so.'

'And sir – ' Tildesley blushed furiously – 'I'd like – we'd like to say – I mean, to compliment you, sir, on the way you handled her.'

'I take that kindly of you, Mr Tildesley. Wait,' Peard added as the third lieutenant turned to go; he had to nerve himself for the question. 'Can you tell me our losses?'

'Only one man killed, sir – Tasker, at the wheel. Eight wounded. Mr Macaulay has a flesh wound – but you're hurt yourself, sir. Look at your stick.'

The blood from his wounded shoulder, Peard saw, had run

down over his hand and down the stick to form a small pool.

'Nothing to worry about, Mr Tildesley,' he said. 'And as for the stick, I believe I can manage without it now.'

He limped to the rail and cast the stick far into the grey water.

CHAPTER SEVEN
The Running Fight

1

Bonaparte's star was in the ascendant. Withdrawing from his untenable position in Syria, the indestructible soldier of the Republic had routed an army of 15,000 Turks landed by a British squadron at Aboukir and returned to Paris, there to give his country a new constitution with himself as First Consul. It was reported that his next move would be the conquest of all Italy. A British army had been defeated in Holland, powerful French and Spanish fleets had united at Cadiz, and at home in England two harvest failures in succession had brought the country to the verge of famine.

To Malta, far away on the rim of these happenings, the frigate *Penelope* brought the news of them. And *Penelope* was just in time to assist *Lion* and *Foudroyant* in the capture of *Guillaume Tell*, when the French 80-gun ship made her desperate attempt to reach Toulon from her Valletta refuge four weeks after the taking of *Généreux*. Neither Rear-Admiral Nelson nor Captain Shuldham Peard took part in this. Nelson, assigned by Lord Keith to the command of the ships blockading Valletta, had refused; 'I could no more stay fourteen days longer here than fourteen years,' he wrote. So, relieved of his Mediterranean command, he was on his way back to England with the Hamiltons, leaving *Foudroyant* to be commanded by Captain Sir Edward Berry. As for Captain Peard, he was occupied in repairing his battered frigate.

Success had suffered worse punishment than had at first been

apparent. Her ageing timbers, subjected to the full force of
Généreux's broadside, needed more attention than could be
given while she was afloat and with some difficulty and hazard
(her pumps manned continuously) she had been brought into
the small bay of Marsa Scirocco where she could be lightened
of guns and stores and her waterline planking got at. Through
the brilliant spring days they worked on her, assisted by
Maltese volunteers from the neighbouring township of
Birzebuggia, while six miles away General Vaubois and his
4,000 men starved and sweltered in their beleaguered fortress.

The siege of Valletta had lasted for nearly two years now.
Since the failed attack of New Year's Day 1799 there had been
an abortive skirmish or two, but Major-General Pigot saw no
point in sacrificing his men in useless assaults when all he had
to do was to pen the French within their walls on the
landward side while the blockade sealed off their supply route
to seaward. Sooner or later they must surrender. Though the
troopships of the relief expedition had escaped and returned to
Toulon, the armed storeship *Ville de Paris* had been taken by
Northumberland (a welcome access of supplies for the needy
Maltese) and Vaubois could abandon hope of further
attempts to relieve him; that he had ordered *Guillaume Tell* to
make her dash for safety seemed to indicate that he had done
so. Yet still the Tricouleur flaunted on the Valletta ramparts.

Captain Peard, limping here and there on his supervision of
repairs, thought sometimes of Julia Vitale within those walls
and was sorry for her. He felt no other emotion towards her,
though he wondered – without rancour – whether Captain
Jean Gagneraud was her lover now. It was Gagneraud,
curiously enough, who woke a spark of resentment in him that
had nothing to do (at least, so he told himself) with the
Frenchman's conjectured relations with Julia. He still
remembered the effective, almost contemptuous, dismissal of
Success by *Diane* when he had encountered Gagneraud off
Valletta more than eighteen months ago, and was surprised to
find that swift defeat still rankling. The chance of avenging it
would be denied him, for the two frigates remaining in Grand

Harbour would never come out while the 74's patrolled the approaches to Valletta. In his newly-regained equability he could sympathize with Gagneraud, a fighting frigate-captain cooped-up in harbour and doomed to surrender without striking a blow.

But if Peard's mind had recovered from its wounds as his body mended, it still retained the knowledge of his lapse. He shrank from meeting Alexander Ball and Emmanuele Vitale again, knowing what his own honesty would demand. To Ball at least he would have to confess his fault. The prospect daunted him, not because of the well-deserved censure he might expect but because he feared to lose Ball's friendship.

He had learned that *Penelope* had brought an interim appointment from London naming Captain Ball Governor of Malta – Commodore no more, since he had no squadron under his command – and that Governor Ball, with Emmanuele Vitale as his right-hand man, now exercised his authority from a mansion in the old capital of Mdina. From here he had addressed a brief letter to Captain Peard at Marsa Scirocco congratulating him on *Success*'s part in the taking of *Généreux* and hoping for an early meeting. His second note had been an invitation to dine at what he called (with triple underlining) 'My Excellency's Gubernatorial Palace,' and this Peard had declined on the thin grounds that the rigging of his new maintopmast required his constant supervision. There was no formality at all about Ball's third missive and as *Success* was all but ready for sea Peard could find no excuse for not complying with its demands:

My dear Shuldham,
I too am busy but not so busy that I cannot find time to renew our acquaintance. Two reasons occur to me for your reluctance to afford me this pleasure. Imprimis, you are unwilling (naturally so, indeed) to meet Vitale. Secundus, Mdina is a dozen rough miles from your present habitat and you are still, I hear, lame from your wound. I nullify both of these by appointing a rendezvous halfway between

our respective quarters and sending a mount (one of the dozen that arrived with Pigot) to convey you thither. You will find your Rosinante awaiting you before the church at Birzebuggia tomorrow at two bells of the forenoon watch. Sergeant Fisk will ride your horse over and stand by to bring it back on your return. For the rendezvous, four miles of westward track will bring you to Zurrieq with a mile to go to another casal, Qrendi, where you will ask the way to Hagar Qim. An approximate pronunciation of the latter name is hadyar keem. The place, I fancy, will astonish you as much as it astonished me when I discovered it.

Alex Ball

Post Scriptum. A frigate captain will hardly take an order from a mere Governor. But I'll remind you, young Shuldham, that I'm still senior to you on the List.

A.B.

Peard felt the blood hot in his face as he read Ball's 'Naturally so, indeed'; he was not proud that once, in his madness, he had been more than anxious to cuckold Emmanuele Vitale. But when he had read the letter to the end he was smiling. The words, no less than the logical planning, so clearly pictured his friend. He would go, of course; and the ordeal of confession loomed less darkly now in his thoughts. It was in a mood approaching cheerfulness that he rode, next morning, up the rough track out of Birzebuggia.

Spring had moved into summer, but the sun in the clear blue sky had not yet attained its full heat and glare. The hilly track wound across a shining landscape whose golden-white outlines held folds of colour; the green of bushes in the *weids*, wayside carpets of yellow ranunculus, great slopes of purple-red *sulla* sweeping down to the cliffs beyond which the sea on his left hung like a blue curtain from the bar of the horizon. His mount, a big chestnut mare of placid disposition and easy gait, needed little management until he came to the clustered stone houses of Zurrieq where children played in the shadow of the great church. They smiled and waved when the tall rider in the blue coat and white breeches doffed his hat and called '*Sahha*', but a moment later he heard someone shout his name and they all took it up, cheering and running to him to pat his boots or his horse.

He quieted the dancing mare with some difficulty and kicked her into a canter to outdistance the children who followed him to the outskirts of the *casal*. It was pleasant, if embarrassing, to find one's fame thus gone abroad; in Birzebuggia, he knew, the Maltese firmly believed that *Success* alone had defeated the French relief expedition and won for them the supplies intended for the enemy. 'Our Malta frigate' represented, for them, the assurance of Britain's aid and Malta's future.

His road was now a more hilly track marked only by the deep parallel ruts worn in the limestone by uncounted generations of carts; perhaps, before them, by some sort of prehistoric sledge. To right and left there were shallow pockets of soil where the green of young wheat showed, little fields walled with piled limestone rocks to keep out animals which no longer existed except as remnants of dried meat in Maltese homes. Here and there bent figures toiled in the fields, lonely in the distance; and once, through a gap in the low hills to northward, he glimpsed a moving bar of scarlet — Pigot's soldiers on the march. The marines, he remembered, had all rejoined their various ships on the arrival of the troops. Always the sea hung on his left, with the ridged and rocky ground falling towards it and the hollows of the *weids* fledged with tamarisk and wild fig.

On the crest of a rise where the few houses of Qrendi came in sight ahead he drew rein and sat for a few moments breathing in the cool land-scented air. Strange indeed that he should have come to love Malta, when the island held for him dark memories. But here with the windflowers at his horse's feet nodding crimson heads in the sunlight, the blue ambience of sea and sky around him, he was very far from the candle-light of Tal-Marfa under its lowering crags. That was behind him now.

There were few people about in Qrendi and he was thankful to find himself unrecognised. A lean and dignified ancient answered his inquiry for Hagar Qim by taking his horse's bridle and leading him along a rocky path. When the old man stopped and pointed Peard saw a distant jumble of huge rocks on a rim overlooking the vast sea-plain that reached to the clear horizon.

He thanked his guide and rode on, noting as he came closer that the rocks were hewn monoliths regularly arranged and that there was a horse tethered near them. He dismounted and tethered his own mount without seeing anything of the other rider, but as he advanced between two ten-foot pillars that might once have been part of a doorway Captain Ball's long countenance showed itself some three feet above the stone slabs of the floor, peering round the corner of a fallen block.

Ball got to his feet, gave his knees a perfunctory dusting, and came forward with outstretched hand.

'Peard!' he said, and there was no doubting his pleasure. 'Well met indeed.' His keen grey eyes surveyed his friend from top to toe. 'You've reduced your tonnage, by Jupiter! And the French didn't spare your beauty, either. How fares the leg?'

'Well enough,' said Peard, returning his grip. 'Ought I to address you as "your excellency"?' he added with a smile.

Ball chuckled. 'The title's *de jure* rather than *de facto*. Save your eleven-gun salute until Vaubois has surrendered, Shuldham. And *Success*?'

'Repairs nearing completion. I've two wounded ashore in Birzebuggia but the rest are fit for duty and so is my sailing-master.'

'Ready for sea – when?'

'Four days.'

'The sooner the better,' said Ball; he hesitated a moment, his high forehead wrinkling. 'I'll confess I'm worried, Peard. If this fellow Bonaparte – First Consul he calls himself now – if he strikes south to Italy he'll go for the ports, Genoa and Naples and the rest. He could bring the combined fleets in through the Straits, and you know how few ships we have in the Mediterranean at this moment. I foresee Keith's squadrons haled away to the north – every ship, and the Malta blockade to go hang.'

Peard frowned. 'But surely Vaubois will have surrendered before that can happen?'

'Don't depend on it. The French in Valletta have won my respect. My information is they're nigh on starving but resolute to hold out. No – if Keith lifts the blockade and supplies get in from Toulon it could be another year before Malta is ours. – But devil take the future!' Ball's tone lightened suddenly. 'Here we are in Hagar Qim, Peard, where at least two antiquaries of my acquaintance would give their souls to be, and we waste time on Keith and Bonaparte. Is it not a wonderful place? Let me show you.'

He led the way into the maze of monoliths and dolmens, treading a pavement of slabs where small bright flowers grew in the cracks. The great square pillars around them glowed in the sunlight as if lit from within.

'There was a big main building, d'you see,' said Ball, now the dedicated archaeologist, 'and outlying smaller ones. I was searching for inscriptions when you arrived but there's never a one to be found. At a guess, Hagar Qim was built thirty centuries ago, perhaps more.'

'As a temple?' Peard suggested.

'Who knows? But certainly – ' Ball, his eye on his friend, checked himself for a moment – 'certainly not a temple of Venus – or of Calypso.'

There was a long pause before Peard spoke.

'That is my cue, I believe,' he said evenly. 'I have something to tell that you should know.'

'Then let's sit down.' Ball patted a big fallen block. 'The rock is warm and your tale may be long.'

'It's short. Alex. But not so short that I wouldn't wish it shorter.'

They sat on the block, facing out to sea. Above the grey-green sage that fringed the gap between two columns a little craggy islet lay far out on the blue. Peard fixed his eyes on it and in a cool dispassionate tone made his confession, while his companion sat silent and unmoving. When he had made an end Ball said nothing for some seconds.

'You were at fault indeed,' he said quietly at last. 'But *vestigia nulla retrorsum*, Shuldham – these things are over and done with. And I have it from Sergeant Ragg that it was your action that prevented a much worse disaster.'

'It didn't prevent Jacques and one of his men from being killed.'

'Or you from suffering a longer penalty.' Ball stood up and shook himself. 'I think you shoulder too much blame. Granted the woman won the time of attack from you, there's no saying that this wasn't mere confirmation of what she'd heard. For she'd betrayed us before, Shuldham – Vitale dragged it out of the servant, Maria. That partition wall, d'you see, and her ear to it when we were conferring.' He touched Peard's shoulder lightly with a finger. 'According to Homer, Calypso kept Ulysses on this island for seven years. At least your own servitude was short-lived.'

Peard gave half a laugh and got to his feet. 'No thanks to me, Alex. If Julia hadn't gone over to the French I'd have – '

'There's no virtue in your "if",' Ball cut in quickly. 'As for the fair Julia, she's paying dearly for her sins at this moment, over yonder in Valletta.'

'And her husband?'

'Keeps his feelings to himself. Something of a cold fish, our Viconde. And I fancy he had his suspicions before she left him. He seemed unmoved when our Valletta spy sent news – ' He stopped with a sidelong glance. 'Your own feelings concerning the lady are indifferent now?'

'I'm sorry she should starve,' said Peard. 'That's all.'

'Well, the news is that she's the mistress of a French sea-officer there, captain of the *Diane* frigate.' Ball smote his palms together briskly. 'Hauled of all. Belay and make fast. Speaking of matters more important, what's the state of *Success*'s stores?'

Peard turned to reply, and unconsciously they fell into step side by side, pacing up and down the ancient stone floor of

Hagar Qim as if it had been a quarterdeck. Twenty minutes later, having dealt with a number of matters from stowage of biscuit to the proper cordage for cat-harpings, the new-made Governor noticed this professional idiosyncrasy.

'If only it was good ship's planking underfoot instead of hard unfeeling stone!' he lamented. 'You're the lucky one, Peard. Here am I, as fast ashore as any clerk, while *Alexander*'s away at Naples with Berry in command. *Foudroyant*'s ordered to Minorca, so you'll make your number to *Northumberland* when you return to sea, I presume.'

They moved towards the horses, Ball laying a caressing hand on the great pillars of Hagar Qim as he passed them.

'*Queen Charlotte* hasn't returned from Palermo, then?' Peard said, untethering the mare.

'No. And I'll wager the next we hear from the Admiral is an order for *Northumberland* and *Lion* to join him.' Ball swung himself into the saddle. 'Then there'll be just *Success* to constitute the navy of Malta. Our ways lie together as far as Qrendi,' he added. 'Lead on.'

The narrow path allowed only single-file riding and there was no further talk. Peard rode with his head high and his scarred face set in its old placidity. The last burden had been lifted from his conscience and the noon sunshine seemed unearthly bright. At the first of Qrendi's houses they reined up and shook hands.

'I to my ledgers and proclamations, you to your sheets and halyards,' said Ball with a wry smile. 'Well – good luck to you, captain.'

Peard grinned. 'And to you, your excellency,' he said.

2

The summer drought hung in blistering heat over Malta island, the long cloudless days faded into nights scarcely cooler, and still the flag of the Republic hung limp on its staff above the ramparts of Valletta. Far out on a sea that slept in iridescent haze the blockading vessels moved like ships in a dream, *Northumberland* and *Lion* cruising two leagues offshore and *Success* on her old outer patrol across the Malta Channel. The prophesies and forebodings of Governor Ball seemed to have come to nothing.

The news of Marengo reached Malta a month after the event, brought by the brig *Speedy* which had been delayed by calms. The French, commanded by the First Consul in person, had defeated the Austrian army and nothing stood between the victors and the Italian ports used as British naval bases. *Speedy* carried despatches for Governor Ball and for Captain Bullock of *Northumberland*, and hard on her heels came two large transports escorted by the frigate *Penelope*. When *Success* closed the Malta coast to make her periodical contact with the senior captain she found *Lion, Speedy,* and *Northumberland* in company off St Paul's Bay with the transports closer inshore embarking troops. Obedient to the signal at the 74's yardarm, Peard made haste to report on board.

Captain Bullock, grey-haired and choleric, received him with perfunctory courtesy in *Northumberland*'s stern-cabin and offered him a glass of limejuice.

'It's the only thing I can drink in this God-damned heat,' he said, mopping his brow. 'I'll have an apoplexy if it's no cooler than this where we're going – and that's north, Peard, off Genoa.'

'*Success* as well?' Peard queried, frowning.

'No. You stay, and by God I'm sorry for you.' Bullock splashed more limejuice into his glass. 'The Admiral's orders require *Northumberland* and *Lion* to escort the transports and join him. Pigot's troops are to defend Genoa.'

'Are none being left?'

'Aye – two hundred, Colonel Graham in command.'

Peard stared. 'Two hundred, to contain Vaubois's four thousand?'

'That's what Ball said. He was on board here yesterday, in a devil of a stew. According to him it's a matter of days, even hours, before the Frogs haul down that flag of theirs. Every dog, cat, and rat in Valletta was eaten a fortnight ago, he says, and they've no water.'

'But once they realise there are only two hundred – '

'I know, I know!' Bullock broke in irritably. 'You needn't scowl at me, Peard. I'm obeying orders. I feel for Ball, but Lord Keith's in the right of it. He's scraping the bottom of the barrel, and if he musters ten of the line he'll be lucky. *Penelope*'s gone back already, by the bye.' He picked up a sealed letter and handed it over. 'The Governor left this for you.'

Peard left the letter unopened. He was thinking fast.

'When do you propose to sail?' he asked.

'Soon as the God-damned soldiers are all embarked. Sunset is the time I've given 'em.'

'If you were to delay until nightfall – '

'I'm not delaying a minute longer than I have to, by God!' snapped Bullock. 'D'you realise the French may even now be moving on Genoa?'

'Hear me out, I beg,' Peard said coolly. 'Vaubois can't see what's going on in St Paul's Bay but your ships and transports will be in sight of his lookouts when they're three miles out. After nightfall they won't be seen. There's a good chance Vaubois won't realise the opportunity he's being given, for a day or two at any rate, and a few days may make all the difference between – '

'I see, I see,' Bullock nodded. 'Very well, then, we'll sail an hour after sunset. There's no moon and I'll give orders no lights are to be shown.' He shot a frowning glance at the frigate captain. 'We may bubble 'em about Pigot and his men, but not about the blockade. And there's two forty-gun frigates in Grand Harbour. They may try to run for it.'

'If they do,' said Peard gravely, 'let us hope they meet with *Success*.'

'Eh? Oh, I see – damned good, Peard, damned good!' Bullock's sun-roughened face cracked in a grin as he stood up. 'Can't do anything as witty with *Northumberland* – but I'd give a fortune for one of the cold easterlies that blow off Tyneside. Goodbye, and good luck.'

Peard returned to his own ship, opening Ball's letter as he sat in the sternsheets of the cutter. It was a brief and hurried scrawl:

Peard: I give Vaubois a week and no more. Patrol inshore and let nothing pass, in or out. A.B.

He gave the orders that got *Success* under way again somewhat abstractedly, and when she had dipped her ensign to *Northumberland* and was on an easterly course he limped up and down his quarterdeck deep in thought. The watchers in Valletta had been accustomed for weeks to the sight of two large ships passing to and fro between them and the horizon. If, instead, they now saw a solitary frigate on the same duty, would they not at once deduce that she was the only blockading vessel left? *Diane* and *Justice* might then be ordered to sea and *Success* would engage one or both. He had to repress his hope that this might happen; the two frigates would be of great value to Keith's much-reduced fleet and it was desirable that they should be captured intact when the French capitulated.

There was another inference that might be drawn from *Success*'s sudden appearance alone before the forts. She might be taken for a decoy. Whether Ball's certainty of surrender within a week was justified or not, Vaubois wouldn't know of it; he could tell himself that the British were impatient to lay hands on his two remaining ships and to that end had laid an ambush, their larger warships lurking inshore along the coast while a 32-gun frigate provided the bait. That impression should be encouraged, he decided. There were still two hours of daylight left. He summoned his three officers.

'You've no doubt perceived our situation, gentlemen,' he said in his old genial manner. '*Success* is to do duty as a blockading squadron. I'm sure you'd wish the frigates in Grand Harbour to come out but our task is to keep them in.'

'If they did come out, sir,' said Fossett, 'we'd have the heels of both of 'em, forty guns or not. That's if we had more wind than a baby's breath,' he added, glancing aloft at the scarcely-filled sails.

'Mr Macaulay opines there's a fresh southerly on the way, sir,' put in Wrench hopefully.

Peard smiled. 'The same being a fair wind for a vessel leaving Grand Harbour, Mr Wrench? That may be. In a little while we'll see whether they're still awake on the ramparts.' He spoke more briskly. 'From now on I want this vessel ready for action apart from loading and running out – all on a split yarn, Mr Fossett.'

'Aye aye, sir.'

'Mr Wrench, you and Mr Shorrocks will inspect all guns. See that the tackles and breechings are sound. Mr Tildesley, I want all idlers set to the chipping and sorting of shot. Be sure, if you please, that the balls in the nettings are truly spherical and free from rust.'

This access of activity during the last dog-watch led to some speculation for'ard. Sheehy, able seaman, assisting Boyce in the splicing of a new breeching on number four gun, opined that a cutting-out expedition into Grand Harbour was planned.

'Don't talk so bloody silly,' Boyce growled. 'Peardy ain't a fool. Ever since 'e come back 'e's got to 'ave this craft tiggerty-boo from truck to keelson, an' that's all about it.'

'Mebbe he's after getting th' office from *Northumberland*,' Sheehy suggested, 'consarning a Frinch store-ship bound for Malta. Thim's the treasures for prizes, Jack! Holds a-busting with wine – '

'Prizes!' said Boyce scornfully; he spat, carefully, overside to leeward. 'We'll never see a prize this bloody cruise. Stuck out 'ere we'll be, till Monseer Voboy strikes 'is colours. Gawd! Might as well be ashore with pore Fuller.'

'Fuller's got a 'ook rigged where 'is 'and was,' put in a man who was tightening a ringbolt at the next gun. 'A Malt did it for 'im, workin' to a pattern Peardy give 'im – '

'Belay that gab, there,' rapped Wrench, striding along the row of guns with the gunner. 'And Mr Shorrocks,' he continued their conversation as they walked on, 'you'd best put a quill down all touch-holes.'

'Aye aye, sir,' said Shorrocks. 'There's action toward, I take it. With a French frigate, maybe?'

'Not in Grand Harbour, anyway,' Wrench returned.

'God send they come out!' said Mr Shorrocks fervently.

Peard, on the quarterdeck, watched Dragut Point, three miles away on the starboard bow, slide slowly back to reveal the full height of St Elmo fort north of the Grand Harbour entrance. Behind the point was the narrow mouth of Marsamuscett with a mile of high fortified wall stretching away inland to the corner of St Michael's Bastion. The memory of that black night twenty months ago was less poignant now. *Success* had been closing the land on a long diagonal, and now he ordered the helm another point to starboard. Fine on the bow, the lofty portals of Grand Harbour rose from a sea hardly rippled by the faint westerly breeze, their turrets and bastions gilded by the westering sun and mirrored in the water. Two miles, perhaps less. With his glass he tried to make out the shipping in the harbour, but the low sunlight was against him and he could see nothing.

A puff of smoke broke from high on St Elmo, followed several seconds later by the deep *boom* of the discharge. The shot raised a jet of white water a cable-length short of the frigate.

'Sheets, for'ard there. Quartermaster, larboard helm. Steady.'

Success wore, bringing the wind on her starboard quarter, and headed away. Twenty minutes later she came about close-hauled and repeated the manoeuvre, keeping her distance this time and provoking no second shot. From the ramparts up there they could throw a 64-pound ball the better part of two miles, and a lucky hit could put paid to the blockade of Valletta. Twice more she advanced and retreated, while the ramparts darkened against a sunset sky, and then Peard set her on the patrolling course he had decided on, a ten-mile shuttle three miles out from the north-east coast.

He had doubled his masthead lookouts, choosing men who had proved in the past to possess good night-sight, and the starshine from a clear sky gave fair visibility. But nothing was sighted that night, and in the morning he continued the same patrol. The afternoon watch brought the change of wind Macaulay had prophesied, backing southerly and rising to a strong breeze. The sun dimmed and at length vanished behind a spread of low cloud that covered the whole sky, promising a dark night to come.

Over his noon bever of salt beef and biscuit and wine Peard had been trying to put himself in the place of General Vaubois, for which mental exercise he had to make a preliminary assumption: that Ball was right and Vaubois was preparing to surrender. Vaubois, then, would certainly try to free two valuable frigates for the service of his country; he could not be sure (and *Success*'s behaviour could have added to his uncertainty) that two ships of the line were not lying in wait out of sight; he would be well aware that a dark night and an offshore wind offered *Diane* and *Justice* their best chance in a desperate dash for freedom. Such a night, in fact, as the coming one promised to be. If they took that chance *Success* was powerless to pen them in Grand Harbour and her presence in the offing would hardly daunt two 40-gun frigates who could put to sea under the protection of the powerful Valletta batteries. She could only do her best to intercept them. Peard considered that problem, weighed the merits of the positions he could take up, and decided that he must try to gain the advantage that surprise could give him.

In the fading light of that afternoon *Success* was far out on a course nor'-nor'-east, and the watchers on the ramparts of St Elmo saw her vanish over the grey horizon. But in the early darkness of a windy evening she came in from eastward, out of sight from Valletta, raising Delimara Point (where, Peard recalled, she had made her Malta landfall two years ago) and heading northward under topsails only, hugging the coast. The dim glow of the binnacle lamp was her only light, and by it Macaulay peered at the chart, from time to time scanning the black loom of the land a mile away on the larboard beam.

'Point Ricasoli west by north two miles,' he said at last.

'Larboard a point,' Peard told the helmsman. 'Hold her thus.'

The frigate crept closer in to the coast, feeling the lee it gave her from the southerly wind. Low against the overcast night sky a darker shape slid slowly out ahead.

'Yon's St Elmo Point, sir, 'tother side Ricasoli,' said Macaulay.

'Very well. Mr Fossett, back the foretopsail, if you please. I shall lie hove-to here, all night if necessary, so take bearings of the point yonder and that hill you can make out on the beam. Kidd and Parrell to the mastheads, Tupper and McIlroy to relieve them at eight bells.'

'Aye aye, sir,' said Fossett. 'What's the chances they'll come out, sir?'

'Let's say evens,' Peard returned. 'But you may tell the lookouts it's a certainty. You're ready to make sail at a moment's notice?'

'All on a split yarn as you said, sir, royals and topgallants.'

'Very well, Mr Fossett. I shall turn in now. Call me instantly if anything is sighted.'

Except for a cat-nap snatched while Malta was out of sight, Peard had had no sleep for twenty-four hours. His mind was at rest, for there was nothing more to do but await the event; and he dropped into sleep the moment he lay down on his folding cot. When he woke (it seemed only a second or two later) he struck a light to look at the deckhead chronometer and found it was two hours after midnight. He had given orders that no bells should be struck and no voices raised – *Success* was little more than half-a-mile from the Grand Harbour entrance – and he came on deck of a dark and silent ship.

The little group of figures on the quarterdeck shifted and moved to the lee side as he came up to limp to and fro in the darkness. Now and again the frigate swung a trifle and the wheel creaked as she was brought back; the wind, he thought, had freshened, though here, so close under the land, it was difficult to gauge its strength. At least it was still from the south, fair for *Diane* and *Justice* if they came out. *If* they came out. Despite his recovered equanimity Peard found himself nagged by uncomfortable possibilities as the minutes passed. Suppose the two frigates had sailed while he was out of sight that evening. Suppose Macaulay had mistaken Ras il Gebel for Ricasoli Point and *Success* was lying miles down the coast. Suppose –

'Deck! Deck!' A hoarse call from the masthead. 'Sail comin' out – two sail, sir!'

3

High on the yards, invisible from the deck, they were snapping the thin yarn that held the sails. Canvas flapped and bellied out darkly overhead, then ceased its commotion as the sheets were hauled taut. *Success* quivered and heeled slightly to a beam wind, bore slowly to starboard, and came creeping out of her lair with the wind right aft.

Peard had to master a touch of impatience. Naturally she was slow gathering way with the coast so near to windward, but he pictured his quarries off to a flying start with every sail drawing; in choosing to lie astern of them so as to avoid discovery till the last moment he had given himself a half-mile handicap to start with, and now this distance was increasing. The frigate heeled suddenly to a stronger gust.

'Larboard helm. Steady as you go.'

At his order the frigate brought the wind on her quarter and, leaning now to a strong and steady breeze, began to surge through the black water. Looking ahead from the weather rail he could just discern the blur of a darker shape on the dark water and a glimmering triangle of sails; beyond it a second shape could be guessed at rather than definitely seen. Impossible to gauge the distance with any accuracy but they must be the better part of a mile ahead.

'Mr Fossett, pass the word, if you please. Hands to quarters, all guns load with ball.'

No stirring drum-roll this time, only a sound like a multitude of muffled drums as eighty pairs of feet thudded on the deck with the rush of the gun-crews to their stations. Of a sudden Peard's eye caught the scintillation of lights away on the larboard beam – *Success* had passed Point Ricasoli, and those scattered lights, some of them high above the sea, were on the Valletta forts. Simultaneously there was a succession of little flashes along the frigate's deck as the lengths of slowmatch were ignited. The rumbling of the gun-trucks that had preceded them might not have reached the ears of those in the forts, with this offshore wind, but on so black a night a keen eye could have glimpsed the twinkle of flint and steel.

Success's course in the wake of the French frigates lay diagonally across the mouth of Grand Harbour less than a mile out. It was hardly conceivable that Vaubois would not have mounted lookouts and manned his guns while the frigates came out; and as the thought crossed his mind a brilliant star of fire dazzled and vanished to larboard, followed a few seconds later by another flash and the double report. Peard could not locate the fall of shot but he felt little apprehension; to score a hit in these conditions would require more luck than good gunnery. But *Diane* and *Justice* must be aware, now, that they were pursued.

With some difficulty with his wounded leg he hoisted himself into the mizen shrouds to stare ahead, and the glare of the third discharge from the fort lit briefly the dark shapes of the French ships, one considerably astern of the other. So far as he could tell the distance was undiminished, but he had faith in *Success*'s superior sailing qualities. Sooner or later he would overhaul that rearmost ship, and he hoped she was *Diane*.

There were no more shots from the forts. The lights of Valletta were out of sight astern and the frigate was drawing clear of the coast with a quartering wind that gave her a good eight knots. Peard limped along the deck with a word for the gun-crews.

'She may stand and fight, lads, or she may hold on until we

come board-and-board. Whatever she does, we're going to hit her hard – and fast, mind, fast as you can reload.' He turned as a lanky figure jumped down from the foremast shrouds. 'Mr Fossett?'

'Yes, sir. The vessel astern of t'other – ' Fossett paused to get his breath – 'I reckon she's *Diane*, sir.'

'I trust you're right. We've a score to settle with *Diane*.'

'We have that, sir. And by'r leave, sir, it's beginning to lighten. We're overhauling, but we'd do better with stuns'ls.'

It was already light enough, Peard realised, to see his lieutenant's cadaverous face and the eager gleam under those bushy eyebrows. He could dismiss his reluctance to send men aloft on one of a topman's most hazardous tasks.

'Very well, Mr Fossett. Get the studding-sails on her.'

Under the luminosity spreading from the east the oblongs of canvas that fluttered and tautened at the yardarm ends showed almost white. Their influence was quickly felt. Peard, back on his quarterdeck, watched the vessel ahead grow slowly larger as they came up on her. She too had hoisted studding-sails, but she was not being well handled, yawing off course before the quartering wind; two years without stirring from harbour, without a chance to fire her guns, was a handicap that should help the outgunned *Success*.

Both ships were heading west-northwest, their course for Toulon, and *Justice* was far ahead of her consort. Like enough, Peard thought, both frigates had been ordered to escape to Toulon unscathed if possible; and *Justice* was beyond his reach if escape at all costs was her end. But *Diane* he would have – or know the reason why.

Less than half-a-mile between them now, and the light growing fast. A tossing grey sea under a low grey sky, the Frenchman's brown hull and towers of canvas leaning above the white trail of her wake. The spurt of orange flame from her stern was unexpected; she hadn't used her stern-chaser on that last occasion two years ago. The 8-pounder ball fell dead in line and half-a-cable ahead, and Peard ordered a trifle of larboard helm to take *Success* on a slant to windward, bringing her round on *Diane*'s quarter. A second shot, better ranged, fell just astern of her before the gun ceased to bear.

And now she was creeping up steadily on a course closely parallel to *Diane*'s. Peard went to the taffrail.

'Quarterdeck stations, Mr Busby, if you please,' he said.

Busby's twenty marines trooped up from the after-deck, where they had been standing at ease, and ranged themselves along the quarterdeck rail with their muskets ordered. Peard raised his voice to carry above the rush of the waves alongside.

'Starboard broadside, fire as your guns bear. Independent firing until further orders. Choose your targets and fire on the up-roll.'

On his last word a crackle of shots came from *Diane*'s after-deck, where a row of figures in pale-blue uniforms could be seen, and a white groove appeared in the rail a foot from Peard's right hand.

'You may reply to that, Mr Busby,' he said.

'Yes, sir. Volley, Sergeant.'

'Present!' barked Ragg. 'Fire!'

There was only a short interval between the crash of the marines' muskets and the boom of *Success*'s foremost 12-pounder. Her bowsprit had drawn level with *Diane*'s stern, then her beakhead, and as the rows of gunports began to overlap the cannonade rose from rapid single explosions to a continuous din of gunfire. Powder-smoke stung in Peard's nostrils and billowed across the space between the racing ships, hiding *Diane* from him so that he could not see the effect of his shot, but he could tell that his 12-pounders were firing at twice the rate of the Frenchman's heavier guns. Twice there came the shock and thud of 18-pounder balls striking home on *Success*'s hull, and the twang of parted rigging overhead told of damage aloft; but he knew he must be hitting his opponent harder than that.

Along the deck his gun-crews were a perspective of madly-whirling groups, crouching, hauling, leaping back as the fuming guns recoiled; he could see no dead or wounded there as yet. Close beside him the marines fired, reloaded, fired, with dogged precision. The rail three paces away dissolved in a fountain of white splinters, one of which ripped his hat from his head, and the ball, which passed between two marines without touching them, smashed its way out through the weather rail. That shot had come from one of *Diane*'s midships guns – *Success* was drawing ahead. He had his mouth open to shout the order for spilling wind when there was a frantic yell from Busby and he turned.

Right overhead he saw the tip of *Diane*'s bowsprit swinging across the quarterdeck, narrowly missing the mizen backstay, and the gilded nymph of her figurehead bearing down upon him out of the smoke below it. His first thought was that she had borne up to cross his stern and rake him. But then came a cracked screech from Fossett – 'Her helm's gone, shot away!' – and in the same instant he saw above the smoke the upper part of her foremast topple and fall in a ruin of tangled sails and cordage. She had flown up into the wind, taken aback and unmanageable. Two of her starboard bow guns exploded as *Success* drew clear, but she had begun to make sternway and the shots went wide. Peard roared his orders from the taffrail.

'Hands to the sheets! Stand by to go about – hard a-larboard, quartermaster.'

Success came about in a flurry of white water, heeling until it seemed that her masts with their full burden of canvas must snap. But she righted herself as she came through the wind to lean over on the opposite tack, her main topgallant yard banging loose and severed ropes streaming on the breeze. Peard spared a glance astern for the second French frigate. The western horizon was a dark bar against the grey morning clouds and just below it was a speck of white. *Justice* had made good her escape. He turned to find Fossett panting beside him.

'Three shot in our hull, sir, all above waterline,' he reported, his bony face cracking in a smile. 'And – by God, sir, it's a marvel – only one man wounded.'

'I'm glad to hear it, Mr Fossett,' Peard said. 'But we've not quite finished yet.'

Success's onward rush had carried her nearly half-a-mile beyond *Diane*. Now she was coming back, still with the weather-gauge, her unfired larboard broadside presented. *Diane* was at her mercy, her steering-gear gone, the fallen mast and all its hamper dragging overside, not a gun able to bear on the enemy who in a very few minutes would be in a position to rake her from stem to stern. To the half-deafened crew of the British frigate the silence as she moved forward to deliver the *coup de grâce* seemed breathless, profound. It was broken by a shrill cry, a scream indeed, from Midshipman Hepplewhite.

'She's struck!'

It was true. Down came the Tricouleur, and the storm of cheering on *Success*'s deck went unchecked for a good ten seconds. Two smoke-blackened figures beside the starboard guns performed a species of dance; Boyce and Sheehy were celebrating in advance their share of prize-money from the taking of a fine 40-gun frigate.

At a word from Peard the first lieutenant cut short the uproar. 'Hands to take in sail – jump to it, there! Topmen aloft!'

Success turned into the wind as she came level with her defeated opponent and lay hove-to a musket-shot from her. Her captain had no leisure yet to savour the elation of victory. A prize-crew with Wrench in command was needed, Busby and his marines to guard the prisoners when they were under hatches. Fortunately both cutter and longboat had escaped damage and within five minutes they had been swung out and the men were embarking.

'Your hat, sir,' squeaked Hepplewhite as Peard went to the rail.

'Thank you.' He pulled it on, torn as it was; and remembered a similar occasion twenty-odd years ago that had given disproportionate pleasure to a junior midshipman. 'You may come with me on board the Frenchman, Mr Hepplewhite.'

As the boats pulled across to *Diane* he could discern little damage apart from the fallen mast, which had been shot clean through at half its height. But when he came up the side and stepped over onto the littered deck there was a dead man lying in his blood and a dozen wounded being attended to by their shipmates, while further aft the crew of a dismounted 18-pounder sprawled in a red shambles beside their gun. A crowd of seamen and soldiers, a sullen and emaciated throng, opened to give him passage as he turned to go aft with Hepplewhite at his heels. Behind him the marines were swarming aboard and Busby was shouting orders in execrable French. He limped past the bloody ruin of the gun to where a tall officer stood waiting beside the pile of splintered wreckage that had been his vessel's wheel.

Diane's captain was a man some ten years younger than Peard with dark curling hair above a handsome face that was just now grimly set. His stiff pose and the sword he held made him look as if he was defending the door of the after-cabin just behind him, but he was grasping the sword by the forte of the blade and as Peard advanced he held it out hilt-first.

'Jean Gagneraud, *capitaine de vaisseau*,' he said in flat tones. '*Je me rends, monsieur.*'

Peard doffed his tattered hat. 'I am Shuldham Peard of His Majesty's frigate *Success*,' he replied in French. 'I beg, *monsieur*, that you will retain your sword. The fortune of war left you no choice but to strike your colours.'

Gagneraud's lean cheeks flushed and he smiled slightly. 'That is generous. But this I must say, *monsieur*. I would have fought on to the death had I not had a passenger on board. It was for – '

He stopped abruptly. The door of the after-cabin had opened and Julia Vitale stood in the doorway.

She was dressed in a robe of dark crimson and her dark-brown hair was unbound. Peard's stare was not altogether of surprise, for Gagneraud's words had prepared him for an encounter he had half-expected. He was astonished at himself, amazed that he could ever have felt mad passion for this woman with the slack red mouth and the bold eyes. And though she was a fugitive from a starving garrison she was – he

could not evade it – fat. The momentary qualm of disgust was
for himself, not for her, and his stare lasted a moment only
before he bowed composedly.

'Peard! *C'est toi!*' Julia came swiftly forward, brushing past
Gagneraud. 'Ah, *mon ami*, you come in time to save me. I am
being taken – '

'Pardon me, *madame*,' he interrupted her firmly, stepping
back as she was about to lay her hand on his arm. 'You are in
fact a prisoner. I regret that I have no woman aboard my ship,
but I will have a cabin prepared for you. You will be under
guard, of course, until I can deliver you to the Governor.
Whether he will in turn deliver you to your husband I
cannot – '

'*Sale cochon!*' she spat at him, springing back. 'As soon
would I set foot in Hell as in your cursed ship! I stay here –
and you, Jean, stay with me!'

Captain Gagneraud's face was very red. He rolled his eyes
in a pitiable confusion from Julia, who was clutching his arm,
to Captain Peard, who was slowly rubbing his chin in
deliberation.

'*Soit*,' Peard said at last, nodding amiably. 'You shall stay
here, madame. And Captain Gagneraud, if he will so far
oblige me, may remain on board his ship. Both of you will be
under guard, and you will perceive, *monsieur*, that in these
circumstances I can no longer permit you to keep your sword.'

Gagneraud, even redder in the face, handed it over without
a word. Peard passed it to Midshipman Hepplewhite, who
grinned delightedly as he received it.

'Come, Jean,' snapped Julia.

She turned her back on her captor and went into the cabin.
Gagneraud, following, turned on the threshold as he heard his
name.

'Captain Gagneraud,' Peard said, 'you have my deepest
sympathy.'

4

The sunshine of the late summer afternoon struck in through the open windows of *Success*'s stern-cabin. There came in also, for the light breeze was still southerly, a confused and continuous jangle of noise, as of a thousand smiths beating on a thousand distant anvils. Governor Ball lifted his glass and surveyed the amber glow of the madeira irritably.

'They've been ringing their confounded bells for two days now,' he said. 'Damn their eyes – and their unmusical ears!'

'They've something to ring them for,' said Captain Peard. 'And but for you,' he added, 'they'd be wringing their hands instead.'

Ball grinned. 'You cribbed that pun from Walpole. But you're right – the Maltese deserve a holiday after two years of siege. By Jupiter, Peard, you should have seen 'em! Dancing and singing like bedlamites when Vaubois marched his thousands out to surrender to Tom Graham's two hundred.'

He refilled his glass and Peard's. *Success* swung gently on her cable – she was at her old anchorage in Salina Bay – and the sound of bells loudened for a moment. It came from the belfries of the great churches in Bugibba and Mosta, in Naxxar and Gharghur and far-off Mdina. And in Valletta, where Colonel Graham now had his red-coated sentries on the ramparts, the great bells of St John's cathedral pealed in antiphon to the bells of the ancient capital.

'The French, I suppose, were in a pitiful state,' said Peard.

'The soldiers of the line were. Skeletons, and half of 'em sick or diseased.' Ball sipped madeira and grimaced. 'Vaubois and his senior officers had still some fat on their bones.'

Peard thought of Julia Vitale. She had not starved, nor had Jean Gagneraud.

'I'm told the prisoners sail for Gibraltar in a week's time,' he said, '*Ville de Paris* and *Northumberland* to take them.'

'Yes. And none too soon for me. I've the devil's own task to feed my own people – the people of Malta, I mean – without Vaubois's gluttons.'

'And Madame Vitale goes with them?'

Ball darted a quick glance at his friend. 'She does. Emmanuele Vitale will have nothing to do with her – washes his hands of Julia. *Fatua mulier* is the legal term he applies to his wife, meaning a woman of bad character. He says it gives him the right to repudiate her.' He wagged his head sagely. 'I'd be more charitable. She was merely a woman, and like all women – as Horatius Flaccus knew – *varium et mutabile semper*.'

'Not Lucy,' Peard said quickly.

'Your pardon,' Ball said with a twinkle. 'All except Mrs Shuldham Peard. But it's nations, not women, we should be thinking of at this moment. D'you realise, Peard, that Malta is ours for the taking? – No. That was badly expressed. Malta is ours for the giving.'

Peard grinned. 'And the meaning of that, if you please?'

'I mean that I believe the Maltese will ask Britain to take it. If they do, and Valletta becomes the Navy's Mediterranean base, you and I will have played our parts, young Shuldham.'

'You'd better leave me out of that, Alex,' Peard said with a frown; then his scarred face lightened. 'But I think you may say that *Success* played her part.'

'She did indeed.' The Governor raised his glass. 'We'll drink to her.'

Epilogue

The outer anteroom was crowded enough to make movement to and fro difficult; but the elegantly-dressed men and women who thronged it under the hanging chandeliers seemed content to stand still and talk. The buzz of decorous chatter was stilled at intervals by the opening of a door at the farther end and the loud calling of a name or names by an official in a powdered wig with a long black rod in his hand. At each summons one or sometimes two persons would hastily titivate their cravats or flowered satins and follow the summoner in through the door.

'It's like waiting your turn for the guillotine,' muttered Captain Peard in his wife's ear.

Mrs Peard giggled and then looked grave. 'I think you're talking treason,' she said. 'A presentation to His Majesty compared to those republican tricks – but pray, Shuldham, look and tell me if I'm properly fastened behind.'

Peard craned his neck backwards, avoiding Lucy's elaborate coiffure. 'All soundly belayed, my dear. In any case,' he added, 'it would be *lèse majesté* to show the King your back, charming though it is.'

They were standing in a corner of the room opposite the door, where now the usher appeared to demand in stentorian tones the presence of General Pulteney and his lady. Lucy stood on tiptoe to watch the exit of a stout man in a scarlet coat and an even stouter woman in ill-advised purple.

'How little Tom would love to see this show!' she said. 'But though there's red coats a-plenty I see only one other man in naval blue.'

'That's Charles Digby,' Peard told her. 'He has the *Niobe*, forty guns. If you remember, she was *Diane* before she was bought into the Service.'

Lucy squeezed his arm. 'Of course I remember – it's only two years ago that you took her. Charles Digby owes his *Niobe* to you, darling.'

'That's putting it rather – ' Peard checked himself., his eyes on the crowd. 'My dear,' he went on quickly, 'will you forgive me if I desert you for a moment? There's a man over there I must – '

'Hurry back, then,' said Lucy, taking her hand from his arm.

Peard edged his way towards the centre of the room with more speed than ceremony. Two men in black coats, one tall and one short; the taller with a bald dome of a head in contrast to the other's curly black mop. It was scarcely credible, and their backs were towards him, but he had to make sure. A concentration of gossiping ladies with voluminous skirts brought him to a halt. But the smaller black-coat man had seen him and came twisting through the throng with a wide grin on his round face.

'Boney!' Peard swiftly amended that as he grasped his one-time steward's hand. 'Taddeo Bonici – it's good to see you. But what do you in London, man? And did I see the Viconde with you yonder?'

'Indeed I am with the Viconde, sir. We are an embassy,' said the Maltese proudly. 'As soon as the Peace was signed we sailed for England.'

In his neat coat and spotless cravat he was a different man from the humble servant of three years ago on board *Success*. His English, too, had improved; no doubt Alex Ball had seen to that.

'The Viconde,' he went on, 'is talking now with Lord Whitworth. Afterwards, sir, he will very much wish to meet you, I am sure. Now I must go to him. I am second ambassador, sir, and carry the petition.'

'A petition?'

'I have it here, sir.' Bonici drew from the breast of his coat a small scroll of paper and unrolled it for Peard to see. 'I know well that it will give Captain Peard much pleasure.'

Peard had only time to read the first few lines of neat calligraphy before the trumpet tones of the usher sounded from the doorway.

'The ambassadors from Malta! The ambassadors from Malta!'

With a hasty word of excuse Bonici seized the scroll and darted back to join his senior. But the words Peard had read under the bold heading 'Declaration of Rights of the People of Malta', were firmly imprinted on his memory, and a moment later he was repeating them to Lucy:

Item One. The King of the United Kingdom of Great Britain and Ireland is our Sovereign Lord, and his lawful successors shall, in all times to come, be acknowledged as our lawful Sovereigns.